D1628941

Brandon Donavon was born in a small country town just two hours outside of the city of Sydney where he spent most of his youth. From an early age, Brandon started writing music lyrics that explored the country lifestyle and the idea of love along with having fun as a teenager. Despite his strong passion for writing, Brandon was taken on an alternative career path but maintained his personal writing throughout the years. After a series of life-changing experiences, Brandon decided it was finally time to share his story, reliving his life through a series of books with his first completed novel being *Dead Man Walking*. Brandon is currently completing his second novel *Trained To Kill*. He resides in Sydney with his wife and daughter.

Brandon Donavon

DEAD MAN WALKING

AUSTIN MACAULEY PUBLISHERS™

LONDON • CAMBRIDGE • NEW YORK • SHARJAH

A CIP catalogue record for this title is available from the British
Library.

ISBN 9781528939782 (Paperback)
ISBN 9781528939799 (Hardback)
ISBN 9781528970099 (ePub e-book)

www.austinmacauley.com

First Published (2020)
Austin Macauley Publishers Ltd
25 Canada Square
Canary Wharf
London
E14 5LQ

Many thanks to my family especially my wife, my mother and my sister and friends who supported me.

Also, to my baby daughter as her coming to this world has given me the inspiration to write and again, forgive those who interrupted my life, yet never to forget.

Evil Blood: Victim of Addiction or a Victim of Pure Evil

I am writing this story with the deepest hope that it is able to provide the required insight to help victims of addiction, whether their habit is gambling, drugs or alcohol. Sadly, I had to learn the hardest way possible that the vast majority of addicts live in a harsh dog-eat-dog world, fending only for themselves. They will happily throw you under a bus if it means one more hit of their fixation of choice. Don't be as foolish as I was, addicts know every trick in the book and will manipulate, lie and steal to get their way. They will destroy your life without a second thought, so if you have the chance, cut the ties before it is too late.

The origins of part of this real-life recount go back as early as I can remember. Unfortunately, I had spent the majority of my life (up until the point of my sudden self-awareness) walking blindly unaware to the reality of hidden truths and concealed lies that surrounded me.

Being born the second son was a curse, a true plague from birth that immediately condemned me to a lifetime of misery. Sometimes, I contemplate what the world would've been like if my life had ended early. As a child, I was very sick, having been born with a hole in my head I was diagnosed by several doctors as not living past my early years. Sometimes, I wish I never had recovered from that illness that almost left me for dead. Maybe if I hadn't survived, at least I would not have experienced what I did.

To reach your ultimate rock bottom, to have the entire world fall at your feet, and on top of that have a loved one turn against you, someone who was meant to be your family, your support, well, there is nothing worse We are told by society to forgive; forgive and move on, forgive and forget, don't hold grudges, but to what limit? When will we reach our breaking point where we are unable to forgive anymore? Forgiving to no end is only bound to come with a price.

Having a moment of weakness can be forever damaging. You forgive and they use you. You forgive again and they hurt you. You forgive one more time and they kill you. Allowing someone to creep back into your life after a long history of being destructive, well, that is as much my fault as it is theirs. Never truer has been the saying: "Fool me once, shame on you. Fool me twice, shame on me."

The Money Box

Life is beautiful when you are young and innocent – wide-eyed with big dreams and an even bigger desire to commit yourself to reaching those goals. The world is your oyster, everything is possible, it doesn't even occur to you that there will be obstacles that will try and stop you from reaching your dreams. That's until you are betrayed by those closest to you.

Alex, my only brother, was never around. Being my older brother, I looked up to him and had desperately wanted for us to be the kind of brothers that I had always imagined. Brothers that were best friends, had each other's backs, hung out, played sports together and gossiped about girls. We never came slightly close to this fantasy. Alex always kept his distance, I had suspected that maybe he hated me, or was jealous of me, but I never knew for sure. As a child, I was given a lot of attention due to my illness, so maybe he resented me for that. Maybe he hated the way my parents fussed over me and gave all their attention to making sure that I was okay. It's only natural for an older child to feel resentment once a new baby comes in and takes the limelight off them, but usually they move past it. Alex never did.

Now that's not to say that I thought Alex was a bad person, he had his inner demons, but he wasn't evil. The truth was that I never completely understood him. I don't know why he didn't talk to me, why he pretended like I didn't exist or did everything in his power to make me feel like I didn't belong. Despite all this, I craved his attention and his approval, and sadly that is something that I never received. It wasn't until the first 'incident' that I truly realised how much he couldn't care less about me, or whether I lived or died.

As a kid I, was obsessed with motorbikes, it was my dream to ride a Ducati or a Kawasaki like they did on the racetracks. To drive at top speed on a bright red Ducati, dipping low to the ground at every corner, that vision filled my mind every night before I hopped into bed. I decided that I needed to save. I was going to have a motorbike, even if it meant saving every cent from my weekly allowance. I decided to invest in a moneybox and one day I came across a beautiful big moneybox. It was the largest I had ever seen and towered over me up until the age of 10.

Saving when you're young is surprisingly easy. As your parents support you for food, accommodation and general living costs, you have next to no expenses, so all the money I got from birthdays and losing teeth went straight into my moneybox for my motorcycle fund. Every gold or silver coin that I added to the moneybox was put in there with pride. I felt ecstatic when I threw in crumpled up notes, knowing that I was getting closer and closer to reaching my dreams.

I spent my schooldays daydreaming about the endless possibilities that could exist with my savings. If I saved more, I could buy a motorcycle and a horse, or I could just buy a lot of candy, and all the show bags at the Easter Show. So many options, so many – "Michael. Michael are you paying attention?" My Maths teacher brought me back down to reality, with the thoughts of my money and numerous scenarios still trailing around in my mind. I tried my best to concentrate in class, but it was next to impossible. As soon as I got home every day, I would lift the moneybox and weigh it to see how much it was growing daily. This continued until one day I physically could not lift the box anymore, and then one day, two weeks later, I went to add in a handful of coins that added up to $10, my weekly allowance, and discovered that the moneybox was completely full.

Despite being almost 31 years ago, I still remember so vividly how I felt, being nervous with anticipation at what seemed like the biggest day of my life. I was finally going to be able to unlock the treasure box to my dreams. It was a Saturday, and I was home alone. My mum was out grocery shopping, and my dad had taken my brother to work with him. Being the youngest son was hard. I don't know if it's because my dad favoured my brother, or if being the first son filled him with pride to show Alex off. But then again, maybe I was completely wrong and my dad was just being overprotective, trying to keep me safe from the hazards of the world with the hole in my heart. I had a lonely childhood, missing most days of school due to being terminally ill, lying in bed watching TV and sleeping. So this Saturday was extremely important, it wasn't just any old Saturday at home by myself. This day was the beginning of my new life.

Filled with anticipation, I sized up the towering moneybox with my eyes and deciphered the most appropriate way to open the metallic beast. A can opener. A can opener would be the safest, easiest and most effective tool.

I started pushing the box to its side for easy access. Push, push, push, but it still wouldn't budge. I pushed again, one more time exerting my entire body weight onto the heavy mass. Finally, it toppled over, as did my weak body with it, knocking my head on the edge of the bed as I fell. It was the first time in my life that I experienced pure happiness and excruciating pain at the same time.

Once my body had recovered from the shock of the fall, I got up in excitement and grabbed the can opener, rapidly moving the handle around the top of the moneybox. Turn, crunch, turn, turn, crunch. The aluminium top had finally curved open. Peering my eyes into the gaping opening, my heart dropped. It was empty. Completely empty. Someone had cut a hole in the bottom of the money box, and had carefully reclosed it, to make it appear as though it hadn't been touched. It was Alex, without a doubt, he had taken every last cent of my life savings. We shared a room, I had always noticed him slyly eyeing the box. Every time I proudly added coins or notes to my savings, he would sneak a peek. But I never thought anything of it; I never could have anticipated that my own brother would steal from me.

I sat there on the floor in shock, hundreds of numbers floating around in my head. Being a maths whiz I knew that after three years of saving, I would've been the richest 11-year-old in the world. But sadly, none of that was a possibility anymore, and would never be. My heart was broken, I had been betrayed by my brother, my older sibling who was meant to be my best friend, my protector, instead he turned out to be the complete opposite.

I decided to go tell my father what had happened, he would have to do something to rightfully punish Alex. "Michael, Alex is your brother," my father told me softly. "Blood is the strongest bond that you will ever have, and you should always remember that. Family comes first, you have to forgive him, love him and move on. Alex will learn and will change his behaviour, he just needs you to love him." I listened to my father and decided to let it go. For the peace of mind I confronted Alex, and he refused to admit that it was him that stole the money and has continued to deny that until this day. We became brothers again, but brothers with a distance. We weren't true blood brothers, just brothers by relation. Listening to my father's advice that day was the worst mistake I made, I realised that parents aren't always right. Every single person has their own instinct, and that's what they should listen to. I should never have forgiven Alex; if I hadn't, he would not have been responsible for destroying my life or trying to kill me.

My First Dance with
the Blood Devil

Despite forgiving my brother, I never truly forgot what he had done. I was told to move on and forgive, so I decided to do just that. It wasn't right to hold a grudge against a kid, he was only 13 at the time – he probably didn't know what he did was wrong. Or it had just been a stupid mistake that he would later learn from. The attack on my moneybox was the first blow of loss and fraud, and as it turned out to be, it was a lesson I really should have learnt from.

So, Alex and I grew up, although we had long moved past the 'incident', we never really acted as brothers. With several years having had passed, the hole in my heart had now closed; I was over the moon as finally I would be able to live like a normal human. After all these years of being locked up inside, being a loner who was confined to a life on the couch staring at the television, I would be free. I celebrated too soon as two weeks later, I was diagnosed with another illness. "Michael, I'm really sorry to tell you this." Sitting at the doctors in that cold, stark white room my heart dropped immediately. It was bad news, obviously. "We have discovered a disease in your spine. As it is still very early in its stages, we can operate on it gradually. However, you will need to wear a brace." A few days later, I started high school, with my shiny new brace. Teenagers especially boys are not the kindest specimens, especially to those who are different from them, so as you can imagine I was bullied. Badly. When you look like an aluminium monster that has just escaped from a mental asylum, with metal rods for a strait jacket, people are bound to notice. I was called every name under the sun ranging from angel wings to coat hanger and the extremely catchy 'metal monster'. Five long years I endured of being picked on non-stop. Getting off the bus at school the kids would flock to me to hear what new taunt someone would throw at me, or if I would fall over if enough people laughed. High school was hell, and as hard as it was growing up, it was even worse not having my big brother there to protect me. No, it wasn't because we went to different schools. Sadly enough, we were at the exact same school, and yet Alex did nothing. He would walk by with his friends as I was being teased and do nothing. Not just nothing, but he would act like I didn't exist. "Isn't that your brother?" I heard one of his friends ask him as they walked by.

"Huh?" Alex acted confused, "I don't have a brother." Those words still ring ever so clearly and haunt me even until this day. "I don't have a brother."

As the years went on, I had grown accustomed to the tormenting, it had almost become second nature to me, an ingrained part of my daily routine. It had broken me down so much that I didn't even fight back anymore; I had stopped acknowledging the bullies and pretended as if they simply weren't there. And then one day, my mum told me I would be leaving that school and spending a year at home recovering from a major back operation I was having. "Mike, are you sad to be leaving your friends at school?" my mum asked, as I gazed out the window trying to hide my excitement. A year at home bully-free sounded like an absolute dream. Most of my time was spent recovering in physiotherapy, rebuilding my strength and healing my body. Eventually, I had enough and was ready to be integrated back into the outside world again. Trinity College, that was to be my new home. Having recovered completely from the back disease that caused me to wear the eye-sore of a brace, I was now target free. No name calling, there were girls everywhere, I was a new person, a new identity. The old me had been erased as though it had never existed. I guess you could just call me Michael Bourne!

Although things were starting to pick up in my social life, I still longed for a relationship with Alex. He was my older sibling and I desperately wanted us to be close. So when an opportunity arose for us to work again together, to have a second chance at truly being brothers, I got excited. "He's going to respect me, after all these years, I know it," I told myself every night, convinced that this time things would be different. He's going to be proud to tell everyone that he is my brother. I was 19 years old, had just left school and was starting to find my feet. That's when I got the call.

It was a Sunday night and I had just got home from the gym. "Mikey, it's Alex." I was speechless; in all our years as blood relatives my brother had never called me. "I've got a proposition for you and trust me you're going to want to hear this."

Our Uncle George, a family friend, had approached Alex with what he had described as 'the scheme of the century'. He ran a legit business; he had been running a transportation company for years, one that had grown to the second largest in the country at one stage. Our other Uncle Robert was also involved in transport, he had come from England and was sponsored by a major company to run a part of it.

Uncle George told us how Robert needed 145 trucks and 65 trailers to be washed and detailed – and how he would pay us $60–70 per vehicle. "It's just too good of an opportunity to let slip by," Alex had told me excitedly over the phone. At that rate, doing the math, well it was going to be a gold mine. Back then no one was washing and detailing mass amounts of vehicles like that. It was a foot in the door, and just like Alex, I knew that an opportunity such as that was like finding an oil well smack bang in the middle of your backyard. And that's not even taking into consideration the fact that this would be a part-time gig, where we only worked on weekends. With our eyes full of dollar signs, we started to plan. Putting together an inventory of everything we needed: trucks, wash mats, pumps, cleaning supplies…the list went on until we were certain we had covered everything. Next, we needed to figure out how we would finance the business. Since Alex had bad credit from years and years of debt, I decided that I would borrow $30,000 and we would become partners. I would be the bank, Alex would be the muscle.

Alex would drive the trucks into the yard where I would wash them. When I was done with one, he would bring another and another. With the force of two of us combined, there would be enough helping hands to make some serious cash. We would be the big bosses, enjoying our lives while keeping our day jobs if we wanted to. The promise of fortune and success consumed my mind, I could not wait to start my new life, so I was more than happy to cough up the money to finance our dreams.

Bit by bit inventory items began to get marked off as they arrived.

Trucks tick.

Mats tick.

The remaining equipment was still waiting to be purchased. As I still worked my day job, Alex had to arrange for the payment and pickup of the items. One Tuesday, he showed up at my work and I gave him two checks, signed, ready to be exchanged for the equipment. After work, I waited for him and the equipment to come back. He came back empty handed no equipment.

"Don't worry, Mikey, they're going to deliver it next week." Alex ruffled my hair in reassurance, taking on the role of the older brother that he never was.

"No worries. Could I get a copy of the receipt still, for tax purposes?"

Immediately Alex narrowed his eyes at me and leaned in closer, "Don't you fucking trust me?"

"Of course I do." I said yes, as I didn't think there was anything unusual about $14,000 worth of equipment being delivered later, considering that we would be both profiting well over each $100,000 a year. I had no reason to not trust his word, I told myself, burying any paranoid thoughts. We were in this together, to make money together.

So, I simply stated, "In any case, still just keep the receipts for tax purposes."

One week went by, and then two with Alex avoiding my calls, and not turning up to meetings. Finally, I could not take it any longer, I had to know what was going on.

So, I called our bank manager, Uncle Ted, who was also a family friend, close to my father.

"Uncle Ted, it's Michael. Can you please do a trace on the cheques that were cashed by Alex a few weeks back?" He said he would investigate it and let me know ASAP.

Alex was currently working for the family company which our father was partners in with his brothers, Uncle Harry, Uncle Charlie, and Uncle Jon Marco. Uncle J being the head accountant managed all the company's finances and monitored funds. As time went on, with Alex's pattern of suspicious behaviour, it really made me question if my uncle J really had any brains or common sense at all. If Alex's work ethic towards the family company was anything like the complete unreliable tendencies he displayed towards me, how was it that he hadn't been fired? I considered the possibility that maybe Uncle J turned a blind eye as Alex was my father's favourite son. We lived in a misogynist world where boys were worshipped, and their bad habits were let slide. I just prayed desperately that I was underestimating Alex's loyalty to me, and that he was just busy with other projects.

Despite my attempted optimism, it was difficult to remain positive, especially when Alex was nowhere to be found. Even though we both lived home, he somehow managed to carefully work around my schedule to avoid running into me. When I was home, he wasn't; when he was home, I wasn't. Every now and then he would respond to my frantic messages asking about the equipment with a dismissive 'don't worry little bro, it will be here soon'. I had reached my breaking point. This game of cat-and-mouse had to come to an end.

"Mikey." It was Uncle Greg on the phone, his voice sounded unusually nervous. "Tell me, did you write cash on the cheque?" Instantly my heart dropped, and my throat went dry.

"Fuck." I didn't know what else to say, and Uncle Greg had clearly put the pieces together.

"Your brother cashed the cheques in at a branch." I knew it. I fucking knew it.

Because we lived in a small country town where everyone knew everyone, and no personal matter was private, you would think that it would be impossible for this to occur. However, it was very common for one of us boys to cash a cheque in on behalf of our father, so naturally none of the bank tellers raised a flag. They just thought it to be a typical transaction, like any other day.

Now that I had the proof I needed that Alex had stolen my money, and the bank manager to support me, I went on a mission to chase him down. I was fuming. He had been lying to me this entire time, letting me think that the equipment was coming. He had played me like a complete fool. I decided to calm down and figure out the best strategy to approach this. I knew he would be at a meeting with the family company in the morning, so I decided to wait until then, where it would be impossible for him to avoid my calls. My uncle Harry answered the phone in the morning, and I asked to speak to Alex. "Michael?" Alex sounded tired and worn out.

"Alex, your act is up."

Dead silence, and then he just started sobbing, "It's gone, it's gone." He didn't apologise or try to tell me that he would pay me back all the money he had stolen from me. He just kept repeating two words, "It's gone."

He was still crying hysterically when a customer arrived in my salon, "Alex, I'll call you back." Yes, I was a hairdresser who sadly enough had no love for hair. At the time, it was a cool enough job to pick up; it allowed me to be social and creative at the same time. I had so much lost time due to the years spent overcoming health issues, so my best option was to work in a salon.

After the customer had left, I decided to go see Alex in person and deal with this betrayal face to face. I knew it would take me exactly 10 min from my salon to the family's transport company. This time he wouldn't be able to escape, he would have to own up to what he did and face the music.

I arrived in the warehouse district where the trucks were docked with my heart racing, hands thumping the steering wheel and mind wondering, *How can I hurt him?*

My entire life I had been known as happy, friendly and positive, despite everything I had been through, I was never a violent person. When you're a frail kid who is terminally sick, you manage to slip through the cracks of trouble and violence because everyone feels pity for you. My whole life I had managed to stay away from fights, but now I couldn't think of anything else. Should I run Alex over, or just go tell my dad?

My father Michael senior was the strongest man I knew. However, as time went on, I discovered how inherently weak he truly was. He avoided any issue regarding Alex, who was always in hot water.

Weak, weak, weak, steering clear of any confrontation as to why his son was a menace. I guess he felt he was a failure as a father, since his eldest son had a serious gambling addiction, despite being handed his entire life on a silver platter. My father had spoiled Alex to the bone, and this was his penance. I was a fool for even considering approaching my father, but desperate times, right? So, realising that he would do nothing, I decided to take measures in my own hands.

Driving down the long street where the family business resided, memories came flooding in. Funnily enough both my brother and I had been born on this street, and now here we were about to enter a face-off. My car rolled to a stop, Alex was standing down the end of the street. Standing in plain sight he kept his head down, as though he was waiting to be handed his sentence. Seeing him standing alone with such shame, I felt a sudden moment of weakness. I couldn't physically hurt him, he was my brother. Despite the bank manager's encouragement, I didn't want to press charges.

I knew that doing that would cause pain for the entire family, our reputation would be ruined. My father would never be the same again. Acting in the best interests of my parents, I decided to take the high road and book him into a twelve-week gambling anonymous course. He would recover from his addiction, and then make amends. That's how it worked, I was sure of it. God, how naïve I was.

Twelve weeks passed, and Alex emerged. Was he a changed man? It was hard to tell. He was too preoccupied with facing the embarrassment of discovering that all the relatives knew where he had been. Instead of owning up to it, he just blamed it on the apparent 'stress' that he felt working for the family business. After that, he didn't go back to working for the family for quite some time, and I didn't hear from him for a while.

As time went on, my life started to improve again. With Alex out of my life again everything just got better. My health was the best it had ever been, and I had started a new job in security working for the family business. Alex used to oversee security, but with him MIA, the job was mine for the taking. Security was an industry I had previously attempted to break in to, but due to my spinal disease it just had not been physically possible. Wearing a metal brace had restricted me in so many ways, but now I was free to run, jump, bend, skip and make the most of my body, and for me that meant working hard. No illness could stop me now; I was so proud and worked with heart beating of happiness.

I loved my new job and was keen to take on additional days. As my work ethics were exceptional, and I was a star employee, my request was immediately granted. Several times my uncle let me drive his car home when my father wasn't around, I was building the trust of my family members, proving myself to be the man that my brother wasn't. I had never at any stage intended to replace my brother, but I was grateful for the opportunity and wanted to fit in. So, I maintained this consistent routine of working hard, training and staying sober off drugs and alcohol. My entire life I never drank or did drugs, I had seen what it had done to my brother and I didn't want to follow in his footsteps. I was working hard to stay ahead and focus on getting my life back into order.

A few months later, I got a call from my mother.

"Michael, your brother needs your help. He was found last night trying to take his life. He really needs your support." My mind immediately erased any thoughts of what Alex had done in the past, this was a situation of life or death, money didn't matter. I decided to confront him in person. I knew it wouldn't be a pretty sight as Alex had been jobless for over two and a half years; he was falling to pieces. Seeing him for the first time in over a year, I barely recognised him. With holes in his shirt, dirty feet and an overgrown beard, he appeared homeless. And the stench, oh God, it was as if he hadn't showered in weeks.

"Mikey, my life is in ruins, I can't work for anyone. I can't go back to the company, I just can't do this anymore." He was pathetic, pleading with me, and I took sympathy.

Still to this day I really don't know why I helped him, I should've been smarter. After two times of being screwed over by your own flesh and blood, you would think that I would have learnt. But this was different; this was his life on the line. I prayed that it was the right choice, that supporting him was the right thing to do. If he left this earth, I would never be able to live with myself. Mistake number three.

Alex the Grand Illusion
That Fooled Me

My father was a spineless man. Refusing to acknowledge Alex's ongoing issues was not his only flaw as a parent. Sadly, my eldest sister was also affected by my father's lack of ability to control his kids himself. Having four children was a terribly selfish decision, as he was never really a proper father to any of us, whether it meant over spoiling us, constantly excusing the wrong things we were doing, or ignoring us altogether.

Our eldest sister, Marie, who is now 48 years old, was born out of wedlock, to the extreme disapproval of my father's parents. "What will people think? Having a child before marriage, it's unheard of." They cared more about the opinion of strangers than their own flesh and blood. As a result, to please his parents, my father did not bring Marie home from the hospital the day she was born. Instead, he treated her like she wasn't his own and left my mother's parents to raise her. Even though my mother never confronted my father, I knew that was a decision she would never forgive him for. Even though Marie was never left without money, clothes, cars and any other material items a growing child could need, it was no substitution for the loving, caring support of her own parents.

Marie always felt like an outsider. She spent a lot of her youth confused as to why our parents had abandoned her. My mother's parents had tried to feed her numerous excuses as to why my parents had done what they did, but she didn't believe them. As far as she was concerned, they had left her because they didn't love her. She grew up as a tormented teen, experimenting with drugs and alcohol and running in with the wrong crowd. Still to this day, I feel sorry for Marie, and what my parents made her go through, all in the name of saving face.

So, there was Marie who had separated herself from us remaining siblings, Alex who was addicted to gambling and gallivanting around the city streets, and then me. I was now working security in some of the toughest clubs in Sydney. My health was great; I was getting stronger physically, but despite this I still dreaded any encounters with Alex. Driving home, I would pass by Alex and his deadbeat friends loitering at a service station, fresh from cruising through Kings Cross in their expensive cars. Most likely the result of drug money, I told myself. I never could understand how Alex and their gang survived, barely working but driving in the flashiest cars around.

One day, I overheard my parents talking in the kitchen, in hushed voices so I wouldn't hear.

"It's got to stop, Michael," my mum angrily whispered to my dad, "Alex needs to know that what he's doing isn't okay."

My dad paused, feigning complete confusion. "I don't know what you're talking about. Alex has worked hard to pay off those cars, he's not doing anything wrong."

"Gambling. Gambling and drugs. If you're going to continue to enable his habits, then I'm going to have to do something about it." My mum stormed out of the kitchen. A few days later, everything went back to normal. I guess my mum really didn't want to believe that her little boy was in such hot water. She felt partially responsible, as the way Alex had turned out was both of their faults. As much as my mother would never admit it, she was also instantly charmed by Alex: whenever he would come over with a new bracelet or necklace for her, she would turn a blind eye and just tell him how proud she was of him.

My brother had cast everyone under a spell; they all looked up to him and were inspired by him. Everyone except for me. The entire family now acknowledged that Alex had lost the investment of my money to the bank, because he had been a gambling addict. They moved on and forgave him, as he said he was in remission. He had been to rehab, and now said that he was working on getting better. "Everyone makes mistakes," my aunt told me one day. "It's important to forgive and support your brother now in his time of need." Years later, I found out the truth of what had really happened to that money. An unknown source had anonymously sent me proof that Alex had never really lost the money. He hadn't lost it to gambling; in fact, he used it to live a comfortable life, going on shopping sprees and partying excessively. Living this wild life Alex began to neglect his health and his body. However, he was still as manipulative as ever.

So, when I saw my older brother at what I thought was his lowest point, I was fooled, leaving my parents' business as I was convinced that he needed my help. His unruly appearance, holes in his pants, unshaven beard, and overpowering odour – it was all an act, a circus trick to deceive me into coming to his rescue once again. I was more concerned with my brother's wellbeing that I failed to manage my own, I was focusing on putting him first when really, I should have been paying attention to the fact that my health was going down the drain.

Finding out Alex was suicidal became my entire focus; I spent all my time trying to figure out how to improve his situation. Day and night, I would spend researching or talking to professionals about the various options for people suffering from depression. This preoccupation with Alex's illness was a distraction, a distraction from realising that I was not okay. I was hurting myself, blaming myself for not being a better brother, a better son, and a better friend. Looking in the mirror my reflection showed a clean, shaven, presentable member of society, but that's not how I felt on the inside. My appearance was a façade; my soul was dirty, it was tarnished, and I didn't know how to restore it to a righteous condition. Once I realised I was suffering, on the edge of suicide, I reached out to my family, I made a cry for help. In a moment of extreme desperation, I turned to those who were meant to be closest to me, and in my time of need, I was turned away. I was all alone, no one was there to save me or listen to my pain. Despite always being there for everyone in my family throughout whatever struggle they were going through, when the tables were turned, I was cast away.

The several attempts I made to voice my pain and hurt were shut down, repeatedly. I wasn't just silenced, my tongue was cut from my mouth and removed. My family had disowned me, they couldn't deal with my pleas, so they took the easiest route possible, ignoring and removing me from the family.

I was now branded the black sheep of the family, despite having done nothing wrong. I was in pain, I was struggling, and I was being the evil one. This is where my own kind-hearted decisions stabbed me in the back: deciding to help Alex, focusing on rebuilding the strength of a wolf, allowed him to repair his white sheep identity again. He had fooled me into thinking that he was wanting to take his own life; he played me and manipulated the situation so that he could work his way back again into the family's good books. Meanwhile, I had jeopardised a future at my family's company and a career in security, all in the name of saving that wolf who fooled me with his façade.

Saving the Devil for
My Parents' Love

When Alex and I decided to enter business together, I really thought that the company would succeed. My older brother was very influential, cunning and manipulating, the perfect combination of qualities to achieve success in the business world. Just if he didn't use those qualities against me, we would be fine. At the start of the business's short lifecycle, I was convinced that he really was my big brother, I believed that we were in this together. Little did I know that Alex was in this for himself purely, and for no one else.

The way humans interact with each other is beyond peculiar. We can have all our belongings stolen from a stranger in the street, and we would seek revenge on them, take them to court if possible, and send them to jail. However, if a family member did the same thing, there would be instant forgiveness. Just because it is someone who shares DNA chromosomes with you, we forgive. Is that logical or plain stupidity?

With the amount of blows that Alex had struck me with over my life, I still forgave him. I had, however, started to learn. I would not repeat the same mistakes of allowing him to freely have access to finances, nor would I bail him out of any trouble he had found himself in. Just was the case when he received a bill from a credit company; he borrowed money that he did not have and needed a 'loan'. After losing $14,000 that I never saw again, this time I refused to pay. At first, he was bitter and angry, but when I told him that he couldn't keep on doing this; when I threatened to tell our parents, he backed down.

As I oversaw the finance for the company and managed the bills, I made a point of making Alex fully aware that with his previous lies and tricks, he couldn't be trusted. He had deceived me more than once, and so he agreed that he would steer clear of the money side of the business. He had a problem, and we both knew that he couldn't control himself. In hindsight, the smartest thing really would have been to have had terminated the relationship right there and then, but clearly, I wasn't thinking straight. Little did I know that Alex was still playing dirty, running his own fraudulent games, doing whatever he could to make a little extra money on the side.

Alex was in charge of collecting money, a very simple task, something that required next to no brainpower; customer relations, collecting money and wasting time. You would think a task that easy would be almost impossible to mess up, it was something that he could do and stay out of my face at the same time. That's what you would've expected. Gradually, I got tired of Alex's laziness; he rarely sweated with the staff, refused to take on manual labour because of his 'low blood sugar', which was truthfully another phrase for being overweight. His health had me pity him far more than I should have, and as he was at least 30kg heavier than he should've been, I granted him the freedom to be a slob. Makes no sense at all, does it? He ate himself to that state; he should be doing whatever physical activity he can to get out of it. But no, everyone walked on eggshells around Alex, "Be gentle with your brother," my father would tell me, "he's fragile and has been through a lot." No second thought about what I was going through, or if I was okay. It was always concern for Alex. How is Alex doing? Are you taking care of your brother? Make sure Alex is eating right. Never a question about my life or me; sometimes I wonder if my parents regretted having me, they always treated me as though I was invisible.

On the other side of the scale, my mother was also compassionate about Alex's feelings but deep down would sometimes express to me her thoughts that something wasn't right with her oldest son. As her beliefs of Christianity go far beyond in relating to Alex's and his powers. I would always hear her whisper to me, "We just can't upset Alex, you know, son, bad things happen sometimes when we do." She would never say he was evil as I guess no parent would ever want to admit that they helped create the Devil from their own body.

Things started getting bad between Alex and me when I noticed discrepancies in the inventory. Items were going missing, first small things such as stationary, and then larger objects such as desktop computers and keyboards. I approached Alex one morning, determined to get to the bottom of this. "Missing inventory?" Alex repeated, an extremely convincing look of puzzlement on his face. "I don't know anything about that, sorry bro." And with that I decided to move on, items had stopped disappearing, so maybe there was a chance that I had accidentally undercounted. I was working crazy hours split between various jobs, so it was possible that my mind wasn't the sharpest. I put it down to accountable loss and that was that. Until one Friday morning, I arrived at the warehouse bright and early and noticed something that made me stop dead in my tracks. One of the trucks was missing. There were meant to be nine, but I only counted eight. How was this possible? Where was the other truck? As soon as Alex came into the office I stormed at him. "Where is it Alex? What the hell did you do with it?" I was fuming, how had I not seen this coming from a mile away?

"Calm down Mikey, what are you on about?" Alex stared at me blankly, infuriating me even more.

"You know exactly what I'm talking about. The truck. Where the hell is it?"

"I have no idea, it's not in the warehouse?"

"Don't fucking lie to me Alex. I know you stole it. What did you do with it this time, sell it to pay off another one of your 5,000 credit card bills?" I shook him roughly, hoping that would shake the truth out of him. Instead he just stared at me, the same sneaky, blank look on his face. I knew what he had done, and there was no way in hell that he was going to get away with it. My dad couldn't turn a blind eye this time, it was the family business and there was a truck missing. He had to acknowledge that his own son, his golden child, had stolen from him.

"Not this again," were my father's first words after I relayed to him what had happened. "Mikey you have to stop antagonising your brother. He is working very hard to get himself back into a good place, and he won't be able to do that if you keep on spreading these lies." No one believed me from my immediate family, only my mother, but as you can imagine she refused to take sides. Funny considering how they had both taken the side of my brother my entire life. But when it came to an important issue like this, she didn't want to get involved. Forgive and forget they both preached, those who are in the wrong will learn and will know to never behave that way again. Such a naïve method of parenting, but then again, my parents weren't exactly the poster couple for parenthood. Considering that they wouldn't even bring their eldest daughter, who they had abandoned as a baby, back years later as a united couple, well that speaks for itself. How could they unite and completely forget about their own child, their own flesh and blood? Again, it always came back to what the family thought of them. The way they were perceived to the outer world was worth its weight in gold.

Meanwhile, the real issue was what was going on behind closed doors. My mother had been the victim of years of domestic violence, she had endured non-stop physical and mental abuse by my horrible father, and it was just swept under the rug. Sadly, she never fought back, she never spoke out. My mother stayed with my father because she didn't know anything else, she was convinced she had no other options. Sometimes, I remind myself that when I get frustrated by my mother's terrible judgement, she is the victim of years of manipulation and abuse, years of behaviour that would brainwash her into thinking she wasn't good enough and forcing her to take on the same opinion as my father.

I never really understood until years later why my family had cast me out so swiftly. Why they began to ignore me and started to support Alex. It wasn't jealousy that made me question this, it was pure confusion, I was never even given a chance and I wanted to know why. Our family was strong with values and morals, we were always told to not judge a book by its cover. Yet I was judged harshly, without reason, and branded an immoral outcast immediately. I was never even given a chance; my book was never even looked at or considered. It lay dusty on the shelf, year after year spent waiting for someone to give it a chance. Alex, on the other hand, his book was given great reviews based purely on the cover. One look at the polished cover and they were won over. How was it that no one ever saw through his façade?

Alex's behaviour never improved, I was convinced that there was not a single good bone in his body. One day, he approached me asking to fraudulently borrow money from my parents' house. If only I could've recorded him saying that, my parents would've disowned him once and for all. He was willing to steal from my parents, to get himself in a better position. When he asked that, I saw red instantly. My poor parents, they didn't even know what they were dealing with, they were helpless to Alex's deceitful advances, so I went to the workshop and grabbed a cutting saw. He had to pay. I wasn't even thinking straight; I just knew that he had to pay. He had taken advantage of too many people and this was his time to feel pain. When Alex saw me running out with the saw, he bolted for his life. If I had hurt him with the saw, I would've been incarcerated, and Alex would've been off free; the poor saint attacked by his maniac brother.

I had to try one last time to inform my father of Alex's horrible intentions. Shaking with anger and fear of his reaction, I relayed the story to him. With deep, slow breaths I carefully explained to my dad how Alex planned to rob them of their house mortgage money.

I was dumfounded. Once again, my father shut me down. This time with anger, accusing me of planting lies in his head, and trying to turn the family against each other. "You were a mistake, Michael. You are nothing but trouble and a headache." I really hadn't expected much from doing the right thing, all I wanted was to help my parents from losing their house. But you know how they say shoot the messenger? I should've just let my parents deal with the situation themselves, knowing that no debt that Alex had was ever paid off, well they would've been left on the streets. Not even a thank you or acknowledgement to me of what I was trying to do, or how I was trying to help them. They were on their own now, and they would soon be left to uncover the demon of a child that they called their eldest son.

Garbage Will Never
Rise to the Top

My father used to constantly say to me, "When the snow goes, the shit shows." Well, maybe we should have called Alex the Snow Devil, as he always would have had snow filling his backyard, forever hiding the dirt underneath. Alex's entire being was a façade, an act that fooled most people, except me. You can't imagine what it is like to be the only one who sees the truth behind someone's lies. It's like having the entire world turned upside down and you're the only one who realises that it's not right.

This would be the last year that I would be in business with Alex. It wasn't a decision that was planned, only Alex knew at the time, and yet he kept me out of the loop and made sure that I was the last to know. So, it was the start of the last five years with my brother. Our situation hadn't improved in the slightest. There were no roses just thorns, no rain just an ongoing drought. I still despised my brother secretly, although I kept that to myself. Sometimes I would watch the news on TV where they would be reporting about a plane crash and think, *Well, that's sad that these people died in a plane crash, maybe Alex should have been there on that flight.* I hated that I had such horrible thoughts towards my own brother, but after the hell he had put me through it was impossible not to resent him.

The last year started off quiet, it appears the business was on track and there had been no incidences with Alex in quite a while. Sadly, I was being misled; I did not know that a tsunami was on its way, and that despite being the best swimmer I still would drown. I could not even float, I would drown instantly, being suffocated by the garbage of lies that covered me like a cloak.

It was half way through the year when I started to notice a complete separation in my family. It was as though we were stuck in an endless tennis match of them versus me; my mum the neutral umpire, and me all alone, up against Alex, my dad, my sister and her husband. At this time, my sister and her husband owned and operated one of the largest self-non-franchised businesses in Australia. They had built it from scratch, and as the years progressed it had grown into an empire. My brother spent a lot of time at my sister's business, occasionally helping them and just hanging out. Growing up me and my sister were like best friends, we were all the other had as Alex never did anything for us. So, I could not understand why my sister never came to me for help or ever asked for assistance. Watching them grow closer and closer, it was like witnessing a secret cult arise.

I can still remember the last several months of that year so vividly, till this day they haunt me frequently in terrifying nightmares. My brother was meant to go to America on a holiday for a wedding of one of his in-laws. He informed me that he was going to receive a personal loan funded into the business account. "You know that I can't handle money," Alex explained. "I can't have it in my hands, so please, once the money is funded, can you draw cheques for the holiday?" All the expenses for the holiday including the airfare and spending money was to be made out into cheques in his name. The money arrived, and the cheques were given to Alex, and then he left to go to the United States. As he left, he gave me all the details of what work would come in. The next day was a Monday, a normal workday and I was expecting to receive the jobs and contract that Alex had mentioned... The whole day nothing came in. However, that wasn't unusual as we still had some remaining work to do, and people are usually slow in getting orders out on a Monday. It was mid-morning when a phone call came in. It was a finance company of that use to manage our invoices.

"Where is Alex?" one of the partners rudely asked me.

"He's away," I responded, wondering what the cause was for the harsh tone.

"Do you have access to the invoices?"

"No, I don't. Alex is the assessor and the final invoice clerk."

There was a slight pause on the other end followed by, "Please find original, we need it ASAP."

I was confused. What was the reason for the urgency and impolite attitude? It was just a missing invoice that would turn up somewhere, right? Initially, I didn't think there was anything suspicious about the situation until I searched everywhere for it and found nothing. Everywhere I could think of looking I searched. Even in the garbage, just in case someone had thrown it out by mistake, but still nothing. I was desperate. I had never in my entire life broken into someone else's house, but this was urgent, so with no hesitation I broke into Alex's. No luck, so I searched again. And again. I was starting to pull my hair, trying to figure out where this damn invoice had gone. Then it occurred to me, Alex's car. It was the last place I usually would've thought of looking, but something told me that night to go look there.

With a coat hanger in one hand and a screw driver in the other, I drove to my parents' house at top speed, frantic to get to the bottom of this once and for all. Arriving at midnight, I slowly drove my car to a stop. I didn't want to wake my parents, they would be furious if they knew I had come here to break into Alex's car. Even if I told them the story before finding any evidence, chances were that they wouldn't believe me and would tell me to leave. I snuck around the back to where Alex's car was parked. Growing up I had this bad habit of always locking my keys in the car, so over time I became a pro at breaking into my own car. A skill that really came into use on this day; I must've spent no more than five minutes and then I was in. Easy peasy, no sweat. Alex's car was a mess, it was filled with rubbish and piles of clothes that I slowly sifted through with caution, making sure to thoroughly check every item, down to the smallest pocket. I found nothing of relevance in the main part of the car, so I went to open the boot. Lying there in plain sight was a large garbage bag. Rummaging through the bag I carefully read each document, from one credit card bill to the next, this was a goldmine of evidence. And then finally I came across the holy grail, the fraudulent invoice. Analysing the document, I discovered that Alex had used it to acquire money, which I assumed was to fund his trip. He had lied to me, again, and this time there was an outside party involved. This was serious business; if the money wasn't paid back, Alex would be facing jail time. What kind of a crazy mess had he gotten us into this time?

With the evidence in my hand, I waited anxiously for my mother to wake up. Her face dropped as I explained to her what Alex had done, as she studied the fake invoice. With a cracked voice she spoke softly, "We will have to wait till your father wakes up, but I don't think we have any other choice but to pay it." With barely any funds in the business, we were still quite a fair way off being able to cover the payment. The funds ended up coming from a personal account of my father's that had Alex's inheritance money in it. His inheritance ended up being spent on saving him from becoming a charged criminal. Still to this day, I wish that we had let him receive the charge and punishment that he truly deserved, as my life without him would've been much different. But for my father's sake to maintain his reputation and prevent any embarrassment to the family, it was paid without a second thought. Alex returned from his vacation filled with anger and spite. Despite us being left to deal with the mess of his crime, he wiped his hands of any responsibility and didn't offer a single apology. Instead, he just informed all our immediate family that he wanted out of the business.

I thought that the bright side of Alex's crime was that I would be honoured by my family. I had saved them from a terrible embarrassment and had revealed Alex's true colours. He had lied, stolen and deceived us, and I had the evidence to prove it. But somehow Alex stayed in the family's good books; he twisted the story so that I was to blame. Nothing but more lies and manipulation to keep the family thinking that he was the angel. "I had never seen that invoice before in my life," I overheard him saying at a family function one day. Those words filled me with rage immediately; he was making ME out to be the liar here? If Alex was skilled at anything, it was how to con and manipulate others. If anyone was ever considering a career as a crook, they could be sure to get the most useful tips off him. 'How to Steal, Lie and Cheat Effectively', that would be the title, a step-by-step guide on how to twist any crime you've committed and effectively frame someone else.

I had come to a complete crossroads in my life. Between my family feeding into Alex's lies, and the repercussions of what he had done, I was torn. If I was to go left, I would be branded a liar and a thief, so I went right to clear my name. Unfortunately, it was too late. I had already been branded, and despite me trying to speak my truth, no one would listen, and it couldn't be undone.

In the following years, I began to distance myself from the entire family. I was completely and utterly alone. Life on your own as an adult should mean adventures and independence, but not like this. I had been outcast from my immediate and extended family and was barely living a lonely, sad existence in complete darkness. I spent most of those years working to pay off the debts that I had inherited from Alex's web of lies. Unbelievable, right? But I had no choice as all the transactions had been linked to my name only and I didn't ever want to get bad credit, so I just soldiered on and committed myself until there was not a cent left to pay.

After working non-stop for all those years, I was finally burning out. I had run out of speed and endurance, just like an old steam train. Chuga, chuga, chuga, chug, chug, ch, ch. The train had come to a stop, once and for all. Realising that not only had I lost everything; my family, my money, my reputation, but I also had to pay off the debts that Alex was responsible for left me distraught. It had never been my fault, Alex chose to walk away from a business prematurely, leaving me to shut shop early, swimming in debt. I spent many of the years working drowning in depression, wanting to just hurt myself completely. Not only was I struggling with depression and suicidal thoughts, but at the time I had also been married for several years. When I look back, I wonder if the toll that my behaviour took on both my life and my ex partners was a blessing in disguise. Over several years, I had no support from her to help me through the pain, and finally, after suffering for too long I made the choice to seek help from a counsellor. I just wanted the pain to go away, or to have someone to show me how to deal with it. I spent several months in therapy. Weirdly enough I felt sorry for the therapist as she would cry in her sessions as she listened to me tell my story.

"I am sorry for your tears," I would tell her.

"No, I am truly sorry for your pain. I have never cried in front of a client until now. It is a stressful job, but I am usually able to be more professional and hold myself together better than this. I have heard some terrible stories, and even though you weren't sexually abused or physically beaten, I can feel all the pain and anguish deep in your soul." She was right, I was truly tarnished not only from all the mental abuse Alex had inflicted, but also from the fact of my family supporting his crimes. Well, he had ultimately made them aid and abet to the crime of ruining another person's life. As time went on in therapy, the tears were gradually replaced with a little laughter as I started to understand that one day I would truly get revenge. Not physical revenge of inflicting pain on Alex, but revenge in the freedom of my soul and being able to clear my defamed name. I would win back my parents and family, I would regain the love that had been lost when they were manipulated into thinking I was not the person I was.

Lies Tear Apart the Family and My Heart

So, there I was: disowned, dishonoured and ostracised from my entire family. Left to hang at the stake, nailed there while I bled alone. Despite all being sinners themselves, they each cast their stones; one by one they threw their rocks filled with lies and judgement, completely shattering the man I once had been.

When Alex abandoned the business, for me to break the lease, I had to remove any fixtures that had been added during our time there. The lease was the only thing apart from the business certificate that was registered in Alex's name, as prior to commencing the business he was swimming in bad credit. As a result, all the contracts and loans were placed in my name. With all the negative business interactions and whispers that were going around about Alex and me, the landlord was keen to sell immediately, and with my luck this coincided with me falling ill with shingles. I struggled through the sickness as I didn't want to give the landlord any reason for him not to sign. Despite the incessant rumours circulating, the landlord never voiced any accusations of his own towards me. What he was thinking was a completely different story, and as it seemed by his eagerness to sell, he wanted to wash his hands of our business relationship as quickly as possible. It didn't bother me too much as I knew in my heart that I wasn't a thief, or a drug dealer or fraudster; I was a hardworking, honest man who was going to restore his reputation.

In our business together, Alex had been the main point of contact to the clients and he also was the estimator. He was trained by the best in the business, so you would think that he would have dedicated his time to his trade, rather than being the face of the business. I was basically a ghost to all the clients, majority of them weren't even aware that Alex had a partner. Even when Alex left the business, they would still call and ask for him, even though we were closing shop. From one sibling to the next Alex hopped. It was the second week of March in 2008 when Alex announced he was leaving the business. With no warning or apology, he just told me, "Mary has hired me to work for her company as a transportation manager." Mary, MY Mary, who had been not only my closest sister, but also my best friend my whole life? I didn't understand, she had always had my back when it came to Alex. What lies had he fed her? Why was I being treated like the outcast when I had done nothing wrong? Mary barely acknowledged my existence when she picked up Alex from the factory. She just sat there, parked across the road as though I was a stranger. There was a chance that she resented me for my ex-wife's behaviour, who had started to act very aggressive towards her without reason. Being stuck in a business working 18-hour days, I hadn't gotten the chance to uncover my wife's true colours, it wasn't until it was too late that I realised how bad our marriage really was. For seven years, I worked myself to the bone, believing that I was building a life for my family, but once the business collapsed, I really got to see who she was. So, with my sister and my ex-wife not speaking I guess Mary started to blame me as well. That's where she became vulnerable to Alex's lies and took his side over mine.

So, when Alex announced he was leaving the business to go work with my sister, he immediately packed up and left. It was as though he was never a part of the business; he abandoned ship, leaving all our possessions in the building for me to deal with. I don't know how one person could be so incredibly selfish and nonchalant.

It was a few weeks after Alex and the tensions were high in my family. A few days earlier, my father had announced that I was as good as dead to him, while throwing a beer bottle at my head. I was under extreme stress, not only from my family, but also from in my personal life. I had next to no money, had to sell my vintage motorcycle that I had loved with all my heart, and was also planning on selling my ute. I was selling all my belongings not only to survive, but also because I still had to pay the staff their outstanding wages from the business, plus the loans that had been taken out. It would've been easier to just declare bankruptcy, but then again that would've seriously affected my credit in the long run. Meanwhile, Alex was acting as though he was completely unaccountable for anything to do with the business and had my father, my uncle and my sister acting as his own personal shield. I was completely alone, and a few days later, on Alex's birthday, I began packing up the belongings from the warehouse to take to my parents' house. Feeling incredibly anxious about going there when my presence was clearly unwanted, I walked up to the gates leading to the back-storage sheds. Loud roars of laughter erupted from the house. It sounded as though they were having a party for my brother's birthday, a party that I hadn't been invited to. As hurt as I felt, I was determined to unload the car as quickly as I could and just get out of there. "Ha-ha, yeah, yeah, so funny," their voices got louder and louder, making me feel more and more invisible. Coming back from the shed to pick up the next load I passed by the open patio where everyone was sitting. My brother, his wife, my father, my sister and her husband were all there sitting together having the time of their lives. They seemed to notice me, tired and sweaty from all the heavy lifting, and as they did my father screamed louder and louder, "Alex ha-ha, yeah, yeah, yeah." He obviously wanted to make a point that I wasn't part of the family anymore, and that they were having a great time without me. I spent several hours unloading the truck, two trips back and forth between my parents' house and the warehouse. It was dark when I finished with the final load and I noticed my mother sitting there, her eyes full of sadness as she watched me being treated like a slave. A slave would've been treated better than me, as they didn't even acknowledge

40

my existence. I knew my mother was silently my supporter, having witnessed everything I had been through, and the web of lies that had been spun by Alex to the entire family. However, she was overpowered by the rest of my enemies, unable to speak up in the fear of being branded an accomplice to a thief for giving me the money from my brother's trust. Despite the money being used to bail Alex out of the mess he had gotten himself into, I was still branded a thief. My mother never had a chance at dominating among those wolves I used to call my family, and she couldn't even survive being their sheep. I was so dumbfounded that not even my father or my sister told my brother to come and help unpack the truck. It was his responsibility too, we had been in the business together. I think they were all sadistic and just wanted me to watch me suffer in humiliation and pain. By the time I had finished, I was covered head to toe in dirt and dust, I felt like the world had just collapsed on me. I walked upstairs to the house in complete silence, and as I entered the balcony no one even looked at me or offered me any food or drink. They all just ignored, and I went on my way. I didn't visit my parents for a long time after that.

The next few years were rough. I spent my 30th birthday and the next few Christmases and Easters all alone, while also missing out on all other family events. My sister's first child and his christening as well, I didn't even get an invite. I later found out that she had asked Alex to be the godfather to her first-born boy. Hearing that news broke my heart, my sister had been my best friend, and now she had chosen Alex as a godfather over me? He had completely erased my existence and replaced me in every aspect possible, leaving me to deal with the burden of his mistakes. I had tried again several times to clear my name and prove my innocence, but every time I was immediately shut down, humiliated even further by their laughter and sneers. As my uncle had decided to not take on the debt from the business, I was dumped with loans, contracts and payments that put me in a financial hole. It's funny though, because when it came to Alex's personal debts, he paid them off immediately without any hesitation at all.

I was in a position where I just wanted to clear all the debt once and for all, so I could finally be free of this horrific chapter of my life. I was made to pay all the debt by myself, and over the period of two years working 18-hour days, I finally managed to get debt-free. During this time, I thought about my family non-stop; every day the events of my entire life would circulate around in my head, leaving me to question, "How did I end up here?" By the time I had paid off all my debts, I was physically and mentally exhausted, I had reached the end of my tether and collapsed. Unable to get back to work for a few weeks put a strain on my marriage, with my ex-wife not even offering to go back to work herself to support me through this breakdown. I felt betrayed, she couldn't help me out when I had been giving her everything she had wanted the entire time we had been together. And now, that I really needed a break, being unable to work due to my mental state, she refused to? It was a long time coming, over the years we had begun to drift apart mentally and physically. I had spent years in depression after the business venture with Alex shut down, followed by my family branding me as a thief. I had attempted to commit suicide more times than I can recall and had no one to turn to. I had fallen down a deep well, a bottomless well engulfed in darkness, with slippery walls that made it impossible to climb out. After the last attempt to take my life failed, after I unsuccessfully tried to overdose on a cocktail of pills, I woke up in a daze and decided that my life needed to change. That was when I first decided to visit the therapist, and over the course of a year I ended up visiting her around 30 times. The last few visits revolved primarily around my failing marriage. "What do you want Michael?" my concerned therapist asked.

"I don't know, too much has happened, and she just hasn't been there for me. I have to have a serious talk with her." After attempting to have several discussions with my ex-wife, it became clear that she just wasn't hearing me. One day, I packed my bags, went downstairs and told her, "Sonya, I'm leaving. I've been unhappy for a very long time. I have tried to talk to you about it, but you just don't seem to care."

She looked at me for what seemed like a lifetime, and then with a sigh said, "I agree Michael. I just don't think that we are meant to be with each other. I know you haven't been happy, I haven't been either. I really think that this is the best option." I walked out with my heart hurt, but not broken, as my family had already torn it apart years ago. I just hoped that this was the right decision, and that leaving would help make my life better. I left that day, and I don't know why but I decided to return to my parents' house. I guess being broke and friendless I really didn't have any other options.

Just like a wounded soldier returning from war, I crawled back to my parents, except there were no open arms or celebrations to welcome my arrival. Thankfully, my mother, my only true supporter, would be there for me, even if she was a silent advocate. That was all I needed to have some slight comfort, considering the outrageous amount of damage that Alex had caused to not only my reputation, but also my mother's. Upon my return I began to witness the result of the lies he had been planting all these years, my brother had set the stage for the show of the century, defaming our names in front of a sold-out audience. He slandered and persecuted us as though we were criminals facing a death sentence, having the support of not only my immediate family, but also extended family and friends who came to his aid after he finally became financially successful over the years. Once back at home my father never looked me in the eyes, he never even asked me for a drink as he regularly did every afternoon or asked for a hand around house. To him I was invisible, he acted as though he only had one son, and that son was the angel Alex. He was full of pride, choosing to pay one of his employees to do basic housekeeping and chores, despite knowing that I was free and very capable of assisting him. Prior to the days of our falling out he treated me as the butler, the son and the servant all in one, that was my role and had always been. Even though I was treated as though I didn't exist I was still living under my parents' roof and wanted to show my good intentions. He never asked me, but I still helped and assisted to whatever he needed, no matter how insignificant or unnecessary they may have seemed. I was determined to rebuild my father's trust and confidence so acted as selflessly as I could, hoping to win him over once again.

While working my hardest at getting back in my father's life, something miraculous happened. I found love. If you can manage to find love through all the pain, then you really do your best to embrace it and embrace I did. I had finally found her; she was a colleague from work that I had met one day while I was still with my wife. We had started off as friends, as at the time I was newly separated, so she became a confidant who I spent spilling my heart to about parting with my ex. I would talk to her for hours and hours after finishing work, it just felt so natural and easy. We would sit in the car and talk about our entire lives until the sun rose, even though I was going through a rough time my heart was starting to feel happy again just being around her. Once we parted after our long talks, it occurred to me immediately that I wanted her to be mine, one day she would be my wife and we would stay together for eternity.

Staring Death in the Eyes for the Last Time

Like most of the memories buried far back within the depths of my mind, I managed to survive by simply forcing myself to repress them. When you've lived a life of continuous trauma and abandonment, you start to figure out ways to cope. Masking the problem and bottling it all up inside really does work…for a while. All you need to unhinge all the years of progress you've made at repressing the painful memories is one little trigger. I had been managing, just existing and running through the motions, going through my highs and my lows (mostly lows), until Christmas one year. It was the year 2009 on Christmas day, and my ex-wife, her mother and I had just gotten home from church, where we had lunch, just the three of us. Driving back to the house, we passed a boy and a girl running around the front of their lawn with water guns. With my window rolled down, I heard the girl squeal, "Mike, I'm gonna get you!" as she sprayed the boy in the face. I don't know if my ears were playing tricks on me because it was Christmas and I was feeling nostalgic, but suddenly I saw my sister Mary and myself out on that lawn, chasing each other with water guns like we use to. I felt a tear roll down my left cheek and I pressed my face closer to the glass, so my ex-wife or mother-in-law wouldn't notice. My sister. We had been best friends all our lives, and now she wasn't even talking to me. Back at the house I was a zombie; while we sat and ate I played my childhood memories on a loop, desperately wishing they could be my reality again. If only I could go back, if only. I knew that today my entire family would be at my grandmother's house happily celebrating as a family, a family that I wasn't a part of anymore. It was as if I had never existed to them, and they were more than content to just move on and pretend like they never had another son, another brother, another nephew.

"Michael. Michael!" I slowly turned to my left; my ex-wife was glaring at me, clearly furious.

"I've been asking you the same question for the last five minutes and you have just been sitting there, staring at your food."

"I'm sorry, Sonya, I don't feel well, my back pain has come back. I think I'm going to go to the shop and get some pain meds." I needed an excuse to get out of the house; I had to get away from these people who felt like complete strangers to me. I didn't feel like I belong anywhere, I was an alien in my own house, in my own body. I felt so displaced and miserable; I needed to go for a drive. Getting into the car I realised I didn't have anywhere to go. I had no family, no friends, no regular places I liked to go to. I stared at the steering wheel for a while before just deciding to go to the place I knew best, my parents'. I was at a dead end, I saw no light at the end of the tunnel, and I knew what I had to do. I drove to my parents' house; I decided that I was going to surprise them. This wouldn't be the typical kind of 'show up at the front door after years of absence' surprise; this would be something far more memorable. I would be returning not as the living son they once knew, I would be found as the dead son, the son that had already been dead to them for several years.

****

When I was eight years old, my family went on a vacation to the snow, it was a seven-hour drive outside of Sydney and I was so excited to see white, fluffy powder for the first time. My sister, brother and I had fought over who was going to get which bunk, and finally after we resolved the issue through a fair game of 'Scissors Paper Rock', we decided to go out exploring. Well, it was Alex's idea; my parents had gone out to get some groceries for dinner and left my brother in charge, as he was the eldest out of the three of us. "C'mon, let's go down to the lake, we can try and catch some fish." Always wanting to impress Alex as a kid, who never seemed to want to hang around us 'lame kids', my sister and I were eager to tag along.

Being winter when we arrived at the lake, we were disappointed to discover that it had frozen over completely. I remember looking at it in awe, I had never seen ice covering an area that use to be water like that, it looked so foreign and magical. With the ice ruining any chances we had at fishing Alex decided that we would play a different game. "We're going to have turns at dancing on the ice," he declared, as if we were all skating pros. Rachel and I looked at each wearily, but we didn't want to show Alex we were scared, so we agreed. "Mikey, you're the smallest so you can go first." I looked out onto the glistening ice; it shimmered at me, silently calling my name. Taking the first step out slowly, I stumbled backwards; the ice was slippery and wet. Regaining my balance, I took another step out, I was determined to prove myself to Alex and show that I could dance the best. One step and another, until I was at least eight metres out from the shore. "You have to go further," Alex yelled, "or it won't count." I took another 10 steps out and stopped. I looked around me, the lake was completely empty, it was almost

46

deadly serene. Where was everyone? Why weren't there any other kids playing on the lake like us? My thoughts were interrupted by a slow cracking sound near my feet, I looked down and then – "Mikey! Mikey!" the sound of my mother's voice drifted through my foggy haze. My eyes gradually opened and slowly focused on my mum's extremely concerned face hovering a few centimetres away from mine.

"Mum?" I was confused, I had been at the lake and now back at the holiday house. "What happened?"

"Oh, Michael, we were so worried. You fell through the ice and almost drowned. If it wasn't for a kind man passing by who saw you fall in, you would've died." Having fully regained consciousness I sat up, my dad and Mary were also there, but Alex wasn't.

"Where's Alex?"

My mum paused, looking almost embarrassed by the question, before answering, "He's up in his room, I think this was all a bit too much for him. You know how sensitive he is."

So, I had almost died after listening to Alex's stupid idea, and he couldn't even come and see if I was okay? Thinking about how much I wanted to die that Christmas had brought me back to my childhood, when I had faced death, and my brother showed how much he couldn't care less. This would be for Alex, for him to truly realise how he had killed me himself. All his actions leading up to this point had been pieces of the puzzle that completed my murder plan. If I died, the blood would be forever on his hands, just like it would've been all those years ago when I fell through the ice.

Arriving at my parents' house, I parked a few streets up so that no one would notice me, and snuck around the side, entering through the cellar downstairs where I knew my parents kept their prized possessions: a shotgun and my father's favourite liquor, Johnnie Walker Blue Label. With a shot glass in one hand, and the shotgun in the other I was ready to go. I downed the drink; it gave me the courage I needed to pull the trigger. I put it into my mouth cautiously and squeezed...nothing. My heart racing, I felt disappointed, then stupid. I realised I had forgotten to load bullets into the chamber. My mistake allowed me the time to practise in the mirror, to make sure that it would be right the next time. Shotgun in mouth I stared at myself in the eyes and then pulled. I repeated this action six or seven times until I knew nothing could fail, my execution was perfect. I knew exactly where my arms needed to be to pull the trigger, and I had gotten the placement inside my mouth exact. Now it was time to properly load the gun with the bullets, completing the final stage of what would be my best Christmas ever.

The box was sitting in the bottom compartment of a large grandfather clock, out of sight for safety. Not hidden well enough, I thought to myself. Going to pick up the box I was taken aback, it was wet. Being in the basement, water must've leaked down to the bottom of the house and into the cracks in the clock. Damn, I was hoping that the bullets being wet wouldn't affect them being able to function. Raising the box carefully, I started to walk it over to the table where the shotgun was sitting. Two steps in and the cardboard box collapsed, along with the complete set of 100+ bullets scattering everywhere. If there ever were a tragic black comedy to be made, my life would be the basis for the plot. Determined to not give up on my self-made suicide pact I dropped to my knees and began to pick up the bullets one by one. 1, 2, 3, 4, each bullet that went back into the box represented every time my father had told me I was as good as dead to him. 13, 14, 15, 16, I began counting the amount of times that Alex had let me down in my life. 55, 56, 57, 58, repeatedly I had been called a liar and a thief.

All the horrible memories reminded me of why I needed to do this until all the bullets were safely back in the box, except for one. Holding it up to the light I examined it, this would be my lifesaver, the instrument that would finally put it out of my misery. I held my little trophy close to my heart and then slowly kissed it, and as I did a deafening sound shook the entire house. It was if there had just been an earthquake, however when I looked around after the noise stopped there were no signs of damage. Maybe it was thunder? Shaken, I went to the window and looked outside; sunny skies, no signs of clouds or rain. I was starting to feel as though that noise was not a coincidence, I looked at the tiny bullet that was still in my trembling hand and returned it to the box. Still panicking and reeling from what I had been about to do, I went to wash my face and broke down crying. It felt as though I was lying there on the floor in tears for hours, but it couldn't have been more than a few minutes. After I eventually composed myself, I placed the box back under the grandfather clock where it belonged, and the gun in its cabinet. Then I quickly left the house, vowing to never even think of suicide or harming myself ever again.

Alex in a Nutshell

From an early age I knew that there was something not entirely right with Alex. I just never truly understood how genuinely evil he was, until it was too late. Growing up, Alex was always surrounded by friends; his charm and calm, collected demeanour made him incredibly popular with admirers of both sexes. He knew that he was worshipped, and he took advantage of it, sadly at the expense of others. Towards the end of the year, our school organised a dance for all the seniors in year 12, to celebrate their graduation. Much to the dismay of half the grade, Alex was planning on taking his fling at the time, Tina. Despite only having been together for a few weeks, they already had an extremely tumultuous relationship, constantly fighting in the hallways and causing scenes. Not many people knew this, but Alex was a very jealous person, and had a bad temper to go with it. One afternoon after the last class had finished for the day I was waiting outside for the bus when I heard loud voices coming from behind. "Alex, we weren't doing anything, you're acting crazy!" I turned around to see Tina waving her hands in my brother's face, trying to make him listen to her.

"I know what I saw Tina. That bastard was hitting on you and you were into it, now he's going to pay. No one makes me look like a fool like that." Alex stormed away, heading towards the oval where the football practice was about to start. A small crowd had formed, eager to see if there was going to be a fight. I looked at Tina, her face frozen in Alex's direction, she seemed uncertain of what to do, but run after Alex anyway. Making his way down the hill, Alex began yelling to the group of football jocks. "Elijah! Elijah you're dead." Like a deer in headlights Elijah looked up, startled. When he saw

Alex storming towards him, his face immediately turned pale. No one wanted to mess with Alex; he was the most popular guy in the school and had the ability to completely ruin your life if he wanted to. Standing face-to-face with Alex, Elijah was dwarfed by his height and nervously stammered, "Alex, nothing happened. Tina was just asking about the Biology assignment because she missed class yesterday." Alex silently peered down at Elijah for what seemed like a lifetime, the crowd of kids surrounding were quiet with anticipation. Bringing his face to the point of almost touching Elijah's, Alex asked, "Do you think I'm some kind of idiot?"

The whispers started, causing Elijah to turn a bright shade of crimson. "Of course, not Alex, I'm just trying to tell you the truth. It's all just a misunderstanding—" before Elijah could finish, Alex had turned his back and walked away. Tina looked at me from across the field, I shrugged in response. Maybe he had just decided to let it go, he realised that nothing happened and that he was in the wrong. Unlikely, but that's what I told myself to maintain a peace of mind. Back at home that night Alex was in his usual mood, acting as though nothing had happened at school today and he was enjoying leading the conversation at dinner. I was exhausted from the long day of school and fell asleep immediately after dinner once my head hit the pillow.

The next day at school all the kids were whispering. Elijah didn't show up to class. It was weird, but not completely discerning, I brought it down to what was most likely just a strange coincidence. But then the next day came, and still no Elijah. Had Alex completely scared the wits out of him, for Elijah to just not turn up to school at all? Alex hadn't made any threats, so there was no real reason for Elijah to be worried. I just couldn't shake the uneasy feeling that something bad had happened. I knew my brother; he wasn't the type to let a grudge go easily, for him to just walk off like that in the middle of a confrontation, well, there must have been some ulterior motive. Four days into the school week and Elijah still was absent. There were numerous rumours circulating the school now about what might have happened to him. The teachers told us all that he was sick at home with glandular fever, but we were all sceptical. That afternoon in study period the police showed up at the school. I was in the library researching for my Ancient History assignment when I looked up and saw them walk by the glass doors. I started panicking, what had Alex done? Word got around fast; Alex had been pulled from his Maths class to go to the principal's office, Elijah was missing. He hadn't been home since that day or contacted his parents to let them know where he went. It was as if he had just disappeared. As Alex was still a minor, my parents had to be called in to the school while the police questioned Alex. He complied with all their queries and had a solid alibi (he had come straight home with me after school), so after an hour of light interrogation, he was free to go. When Alex left the office, he turned and winked at me, as if there was some secret we were sharing. I will never forget that wink, as still until this day Elijah has never been found.

It's a scary thought to believe that your own brother may be a sociopath, or perhaps, even a psychopath. But as the years went on, that possibility started to become more of a reality and less of a hypothetical. Alex never showed any genuine remorse for his actions, and he was an amazing actor and manipulator. He had my parents wrapped around his finger, especially my dad who was convinced that he was the golden child. "Why can't you be more like your brother?" my father would ask me when Alex would come home with a sports trophy or medal. I was the more academic type, but my father never recognised my achievements. My English teacher at school once convinced me to let the school submit a story I had written in class, to be a part of an anthology with works from highly respected authors. As a joke, and to shut my teacher up, I decided to submit. A few weeks later, my teacher came rushing into the classroom jumping up and down in joy. "Michael! Michael! Your story was accepted! Your work is going to be published and sold in a bookstore." I was in shock and was over the moon; finally, I would have something physical to show my father of my achievements. When I finally received a copy of the book, I excitedly took it home and presented it to my dad. He looked at it for a split second, then yelled, "What is this garbage," throwing it in the corner. Alex joined in; laughing in my face and declaring that I was a sissy for writing lame stories. I ran off crying, trying to escape the cruel jeering of my own family. That was the first time my own father had truly crushed my spirit. After that day, I never entered anything again and stopped writing stories for a very long time. What was the point? It would never be good enough anyway.

Alex was the second eldest of four kids, but he acted like an only child. Truly narcissistic to the core, it was if he genuinely believed that the entire world revolved around him. Coming home from school, he would demand my mother for his food; if she hadn't made what he liked, he refused to eat. "Alex, you know you're not the only one eating in this house," my mother had told him after he complained about the lasagne she had served. Giving my mother a deathly glare, she turned silent immediately and simply served him a separate dish to the rest of us, or we would all just eat whatever Alex felt like that day. My parents were spineless when it came to his demands, easily giving in to whatever he requested, no matter how extravagant. For his 18th birthday, Alex announced that he was going to throw a party on a yacht, for all his closest friends to celebrate with him. My parents gave each other a look, and for the first time in his life my father spoke up, "Alex, you know we just don't have the money to afford that."

My brother looked at my father sympathetically for a minute and then said, "But Dad, do you really need that third car? If you were to sell it, you could afford to pay for the yacht." A few weeks later, my dad had sold his third car, and Alex, of course got his extravagant party. When my 18th birthday came, my parents completely forgot, despite leaving them hints weeks before. The day came, and I rushed downstairs, expecting to receive a grand welcoming filled with presents. I was convinced they were acting nonchalant because they had planned a surprise and just wanted to make sure I was properly shocked. Well, they succeeded; I sure was confused when I ran to the kitchen on the morning of my birthday to be received by no one. Not one single person looked up at me, let alone wished me happy birthday. Defeated, I walked back up to my room, got ready for school and left silently. I never brought up my birthday, or the fact that it was forgotten. Why would I? It would be a waste of a breath. And people wonder why I had such low self-esteem, being the invisible son of the family.

Despite Alex being the clear favourite, my sister and I still did everything for him. He was our older brother, the popular boy at school, so we naturally looked up to him. The opposite could be said about how he felt towards us. He barely acknowledged us at school, and at home it was only to tell us to 'get out of the way' or 'where's my blue jersey'. He never appreciated any of his siblings, and as the years went on, he somehow managed to value us less and less, even though all I did was get him out of hot water. I was constantly saving him from the series of fraudulent acts he committed throughout his adult life from owing drug kingpin's money for stock he couldn't sell to losing money gambling. Time after time again I was forced to step in and cover the dues he owed to the debt collectors who were chasing him. This cycle would continue over and over, where I was stuck left to pay the bill, to save my brother from imprisonment, or being killed.

All of Alex's life he walked around carrying a violin in his backpack, ready to present the sad sob story of his life through the utmost soft music for all to listen. People listened; they threw money and roses at his feet, crying for him with each stroke of the violin. Why they fell for his façade I never truly understood. If they only knew his true character, they would ask for their pennies and flowers back. Alex was a lazy man, he rarely worked, and when he did it was done with constant complaints. "My back hurts, you know that I shouldn't be doing work like this." The violin played at a low hum. "I'm so bored, I'm far too smart to be doing this kind of work." Slowly the strokes increased to a higher vibration, increasing in intensity. "I'm going to die Mikey, this is work for slaves." The violin exploded, the strings breaking at being strummed too roughly. Poor Alex. He never paid a bill, I don't even know if he would know how if he tried. He relied on his wife to pay all his bills, his wife who considered Alex a saint, not knowing the truth of even half of the things he had done. The amount of times he had borrowed money from me, money that I never saw again, which then graduated into him stealing from not only me, but also our parents. If only his wife knew. Maybe he just had the gift of the gab because when he opened his mouth, people would gather silently and listen. Not that he needed to speak because his image had the ability to tell a story without words. He would wear the same shirt day after day and never look like he was drowning in debt or cared about all the flashy belongings he lusted after. As Alex got older, he gradually became less and less toxic to everyone around him. He had changed, yes, and I do believe that we all deserve second chances. However, this wasn't just a second chance. Alex had used up his second, his third, his 100th chance many years ago. He had been so consumed by lies and deception over the years that he was well past second chances with me. There was no way in this world he could redeem himself; he couldn't turn back time, he could only inform others that his past was his past. And desperately hope to God that it would stay that way.

The Day of Redeeming Myself
Was a Bitch for Others

Years flew by; autumns passed, summers and winters, I had lost count of how many seasons it had been since I had last seen my family. Fast forward to 2018, I now had a wife and a daughter, a family of my own who was my entire world. My years of suicide and depression were behind me; somehow despite reaching my lowest point possible, I had managed to turn things around for myself and really make a change. It is true what they say about how things can only go up once you've hit your rock bottom. Considering my rock bottom was contemplating suicide daily, with numerous failed attempts, there was nowhere else to go but up. It's funny, when you feel like a complete failure and the universe doesn't even let you succeed in killing yourself, you know that there is some plan in store for you. I was meant to move on and have something to live for, and I had finally found it in my wife and child.

That's not to say that the uphill climb was an easy one. I stayed strong and worked through the darkness, but that trek was a rocky one, with jagged rocks that I tripped and fell onto, slicing me on my calves and knees. With blood streaming down my legs I carried on, not determined to let any wounds prevent me from reaching the top. When I climbed, I thought about my past and pain, my mother and father's faces would appear, worn with the ageing of years past. I felt their sadness, their misery at losing their son, yet never truly knowing the extent of my innocence. I thought about my supportive wife and daughter who I lived for, smiling happily in support of my journey. Thinking about all of them carried me through the difficult expedition, until all my pain had disappeared.

Although time had passed, and wounds had healed, I was still an outcast to my family. Knowing that my daughter would never get a chance to know my parents or my siblings because I was branded the devil, well, that was something that I just couldn't sit by and let happen. My beautiful daughter deserved to be loved, appreciated and spoiled just like my wife's family did, and I wanted my family to be a part of that too. I was determined to reclaim my place, restore my reputation and clear my name once and for all. So, I had reached the grand stage, I had come to final hurdle where I had to face my family for the last time.

To fix this mess, I knew that I needed to approach the Uncle who had aided and abetted in my brother's lies, as he had been tricked, like the rest of the family, into believing him. It wasn't his fault, Alex was a sly snake that had fooled everyone, and it was time for that to change. In the interest of not causing any further pain or hurt to anyone I decided to draft a non-disclosure agreement for myself and my uncle, so that the conversation and issues discussed were to remain private. Two days later I went to visit the family business that my uncle ran, which was also my brothers place of work where he was employed as an assessor. There were about 15 stairs leading up to my uncle's office, but it felt like over a thousand, as I walked up to visit the captain of my brother's boat. He was in control of the resolution of this issue, so he needed to know the truth of the past and my brother's wrong doings. If for some unfortunate reason this plan didn't work, then I had formulated a backup plan. Plan B involved me placing a caveat on all my brother's and uncle's assets, hoping that the seriousness of the claim of defamation and slander would make them finally stop and listen.

So, the day before unveiling myself to my uncle, I decided to meet up with Leo, the only cousin that still talked to me. After a four-hour discussion, it became evident that Plan A never was going to work, however, the upside was in those four hours I had gained myself a much-needed alliance.

Throughout the years I had been lost and confused, left in the dark, while the reason for my family's excommunication puzzled me daily. With my new-found ally, the mystery was beginning to unravel, as well as the final piece to the puzzle that I had been in search of for many years. Brainstorming for four hours straight with one of my brother's believers, I was convinced that I was like an apostle who was sitting with Jesus, listening to his words of wisdom. After Leo left I continued to reflect on the years that had passed, and all the perplexities began to clear. All my clouded judgements and doubts regarding who, what, when, why, in an instant I began to understand. Sifting through the memories in my mind, as painful as it was, I started to recall several events that had occurred the year before in 2017.

I began to relive events that I previously was never able to understand; they had been an unsolved mystery so to speak. Mid-2017, my wife and I had been invited to a wedding of one of my cousin's children. Not having seen the family of my uncles and cousins for many years now I knew it would not be an easy event to attend but seeing as now I owned a service company that I had devoted all my time and energy into building, I considered myself to be quite successful, and so I thought, unbreakable. I had wealth to show now, wealth that I had built from the ground up. They had to respect me now, right? So, I arrived at the wedding, nervous, but ready to face my family. I never thought for one minute how worthless I would feel once I left. At the wedding I would be representing my mother and father alongside my sister and her husband. Our family is one of the largest Arabic families in Sydney, with a total of over 150 first blood relatives, let's not even begin to count the second cousins. All my immediate family were there, excluding my brother as he chose not to come at the last minute. I wonder if it was because of me, although he never had previously shied away from any opportunity to make a mockery of me. The wedding was beyond uncomfortable; no one spoke to, acknowledged, drank with, or visited me, or my wife at our table. I even attempted to look around and nod greetings, my eyes wandering desperately as they do when you're at a wedding of over six hundred people. But the only greetings that were reciprocated were with death stares or blatantly turning the other way. Leo was the only person that spoke to me that day. Going home, I was almost in tears.

The next event took place just after my first child, Camila, was born. She was an angel from her mother who changed my life the moment she came into this world. After she was born, the house was buzzing with visitors from my wife's family, who came with gifts and kisses, giving her the love, she deserved entering this world. That, however, was not the case with my family, barely anyone called or sent their best wishes, and only one relative and his family visited as he was one of my father's business partners. He may as well have not even bothered as you could feel through his eyes and energy that he didn't want to be there, the awkward silences felt like torture, making me feel so sad for my beautiful girl. Of course, Leo came to visit with his daughter, bringing their love and laughter, almost making up for that horrible previous visit. The third event that I remembered was my daughter's Christening, where not one single relative outside of my immediate family was invited. As Camila was my first child, in most cultures around the world a Christening would be one of the most important events in a parent's life. So, at the time I decided to approach my father to ask whom I should invite, "Dad, I know that there are difficulties between me and Alex, but I would love for the rest of the family to be there. Who do you think I should invite?"

I recall my father pausing for quite some time before answering me, "For your first child's Christening you should just invite your siblings. Keep it small and intimate." I didn't think that his response was odd at the time, even though it was typical for all relatives to be invited to such monumental events as a Christening. Even if they did not attend it was the polite thing to do to offer them an invite. It wasn't until later that I realised he was sending me a message, he was trying to tell me that no one respected me or my name, and as a result they would not respect the birth of my daughter.

I sat in my office for hours, mulling over what had been revealed to me. How had I never realised any of this before? Bit by bit more pieces of puzzle were falling into place, the facades were being uncovered, the illusions stripped away. It was possible that my immediate family knew of the defamation and slander but never told me. My mind was exhausted, there had been so many strange incidents over the years and I just couldn't make sense of it all, I desperately needed a rest. As I lay my head down looking at my sleeping wife and baby daughter, it suddenly hit me that I wouldn't have a legacy to pass on, not one that I would be proud of anyway. So, the next day I rang my solicitor immediately and put a defamation and slander suit in forward action against my family. This had gone on far too long, they needed to realise they couldn't keep messing with my life anymore. I decided to meet up with Leo again as he had been more than supportive of clearing my name. After explaining to him how I had decided to go ahead with the defamation suit his face dropped. "Mikey, I'm so sorry. I really must apologise now. You know I was a supporter of Alex's lies, I even said a few bad things against you a few times. I don't know why I did it, I didn't even know your side of the story. I just stupidly assumed that you were guilty. I guess if you hear something from someone you're close to you never really stop to question it, you just support it." Hurt and shocked at his sudden confession, I was also grateful that I now had my cousin back on my side.

I gave him a hug, telling him I forgave him, then he suddenly pulled away in anger, "This just makes me so mad. He has everyone convinced that you're the devil when you are basically innocent here. I honestly can't think of anyone that doesn't or hasn't supported your brother and his lies." With more than enough motivation that I needed for one day I decided to print the letter of intent to sue my uncle and brother and go to the family business where I would hand it in immediately. It was already late on a Thursday afternoon when I called the business and spoke to my auntie. "Hello

Auntie, it's Mikey. I'm nearby and want to come in and speak to uncle regarding a bill."

"Hi Mike, yes you can come in now. I will let him know."

"Great, I will be there very soon."

As I arrived at the warehouse, I began to walk up to the office, where I noticed twin brothers standing at the doorway, who still work there from 21 years ago when I was there as an apprentice. With a massive smile, I began waving in acknowledgement and filled with excitement at seeing familiar faces. I was now about 10 metres away and could see them smiling, but my happy thoughts were interrupted by loud noises and screaming erupting from behind me. The twins face turned from joy to immediate disbelief as I heard hostile voices getting closer and closer.

"Hey, what you are doing?" Ten steps away.

"Hey, who are you?" Six steps.

"You can't be there!" Three steps.

"WHO ARE YOU?" I felt as though it was screamed right into my ear.

I turned around suddenly and two guys, who worked with my uncle both looked like they were about to attack me, with their final aggressive, "Who the fuck are you?"

I took my sunglasses off and said, "I am Michael. Michael Beshara, the son of director Michael senior." I spoke with a clenched fist, as one of the men had visited my family home where I lived with my father, mother, wife and baby daughter, and called me an evil twin. I never forget someone who slanders you in your own home. The other manager I met many times and had never had any problems with him.

Upon hearing me state my name, their faces turned white, like ghosts in disbelief. Justin, the name-calling one spoke up, "We were informed that there was a Lebanese customer who was coming to tear shit up. We thought you were him, so sorry, we didn't recognise you." I looked at them suspiciously, as that made no sense at all, I could see my Auntie in the secretary desk, she had been informed that I was coming. Even if she had forgotten to pass the message along that I was making a visit, why wouldn't my cousin come out here first to check if my body language or actions looked threatening? Why didn't they inform my uncle who was upstairs prior that a disgruntle customer was approaching? Even if it was a case of mistaken identity, why would I be approached by two employees of a business who never deal in customer relations, who despite not having seen me for a long time, still managed to recognise me from distance. If I was there planning to tear shit up as a disgruntled customer wouldn't I just go directly to the office where all the management was located. I just don't know, it didn't make any sense. Perhaps the unknown would never be revealed in this situation.

So, there I was at my lowest, I finally felt like a dead man walking as there was nothing else that could ever destroy me like the incident I was just in. My many conversations with Leo had helped me to discover that we all wear many hats in life. I was in a position where I needed to take that advice and choose the right hat for the current situation. In the past I would have screamed and caused a crazy scene. Tearing shit up would be an understatement. So, with the correct hat chosen I just walked away from my two attackers, directing myself back to the office to proceed with the initial plan: pay the bill I owed and hand my uncle the letter. As I entered the office, both of my attackers from the previous incident were standing there, guilty looks covering both of their faces.

Justin walked towards me, both hands held out, "Michael, I am truly sorry. I thought you were a customer planning to tear shit up."

My auntie was sitting at the reception desk and I called out to her, "Auntie, this guy comes to my house and calls me an evil son, but he can't recognise me. How does that make sense?"

Stunned, yet trying to act aloof, my auntie replied, "I didn't know where they went when they left the office."

"You know what? I really don't care anymore." I sighed, turned to the manager and said, "Mate apology accepted." Then I looked over to my auntie, who still looked surprised and told her, "No sweat off my back, I have been ostracized all my life within this business, and this family, so I don't really care anymore. I'm over it." She stared at me blankly and didn't even offer me an apology or a drink for the incident that had just occurred. She didn't even suggest to informing her son to take me around to meet all the new staff to introduce me so that something like that didn't ever happen again. They all just stood there silently, acting as though nothing had happened. Of course, I don't even have to mention that they are close with my brother, Alex. With that said, I paid the bill, left and went upstairs to hand my uncle the letter. As I left I said only a few words to my uncle as I handed him the fateful letter, "Have a good day, have a good day."

Waiting to Be Sentenced

Back at home that evening, I sat nervously in silence, biting my nails and staring at my phone. Not one single phone call, how had there not been an uproar already in response to my letter? Maybe my phone wasn't working. I tried calling my mobile from my wife's phone. It rang. Frustrated, I let out a sigh, then collapsed back in the same chair again, where I sat, twitching, just waiting. "Michael, you have to get out of that chair and stop stressing yourself. It's making me nervous just watching you!" My wife stood there, exasperated at the madness I was clearly experiencing the past few hours. "I'm sorry darling, I will try and let it go for now. Let's try to get some sleep." Pointless words, as I barely slept that night, instead I lay wide awake staring at the ceiling, thousands of scenarios running through my mind as to why no one had contacted me.

When the morning finally came, I had to go to the bank to pick up over 1,000 pages of statements to go through for evidence. On the way there I called my solicitor, "Mark, it's Mikey. Any word from my uncle?"

"Yeah." A pause and then a chuckle of disbelief, "That bastard isn't taking this seriously. He commented on the letter, texted a photo and then threatened to go to police. Below the signature and date on your letter he wrote, *You're a little late for April fools*."

Once I heard this, I was filled with rage. My uncle was making a mockery of my pain, the one who had been Alex's primary supporter laughed in response to my serious letter of intent.

His reply showed not only a lack of compassion, but also demonstrated that he had no understanding of my pain at all, making a joke out of my letter that had gone into detail about my depression and suicide attempts. What kind of cruel, heartless person makes a joke out of another person's misery, especially when they are blood relatives?

"I didn't know it was April fools!" The words circled around in my head, until I was dizzy with rage. Uttering 1,000 curses on my uncle's soul, I went to pick up the phone, trembling from the overpowering anger. He had started a war, I had given him the opportunity to address this like adults and he had laughed in my face. Punching in the numbers into the phone I waited for his reply. "Uncle. You are nothing to me, you laugh at my pain? You think that a man being depressed and on the verge of suicide is funny? This is how you respond to a cry for help? You have no idea what you have just done, but you'll soon find out." Not waiting to hear a response I hung up immediately. I didn't care what he had to say, I had one more person to deal with, my brother. "Alex. You have stripped out my soul, you have ruined my life. I am sick of your lies and covering up your crimes for you. I am fucking done. You better get fucking ready because I am going to reveal who you really are once and for all." My wife stood in shock in my parents' kitchen watching her husband slowly becoming a beast, a stranger that she didn't know. She had never experienced or witnessed me in a state of absolute rage. For a second, I saw a glimpse of fear in her eyes, and that made me even angrier. This was the person my brother had turned me into, and with that thought I screamed at him even louder, drowning out his threats and his desperate claims of denial.

"Mikey, you better watch out. I'm going to come there right now and fix you right up. You won't be able to say another word after I'm done with you." How dare he threaten to come to my house where I lived with my parents and family? How dare he threaten my home with violence? I was prepared for war; war and collateral damage that Alex would never experience in his lifetime. I was no longer thinking about the blood running through my veins, all I could focus on was the thought of blood spilling from the wounds that I would be inflicting all over Alex's body. I wanted to watch him die; I needed to watch him suffer just as he had mercilessly made me suffer for years on end. Living in Australia, guns aren't a common household possession, but at this stage I wish I could get my hands on one. I protected my family home as it was my fortress and I was the warrior guarding the gate.

Preparing for battle, there were two weapons I needed by my side; Priscilla and Bethany, one was a wooden baseball bat, the other, an axe. Running to get them I grabbed the phone and started to call the police. Ring ring, ring ring – I hung up, what the hell was I doing? If Alex took things too far this time, who knows how I might react. My blood was boiling, I was seeing red, yet a faint voice in my head told me to be smart and not get the authorities involved. There was a very high possibility that blood would be shed tonight, and if the police arrived at the wrong time while I was trying to protect my family from an intruder, even if it was my brother, well that would end very badly for me. Unless I could prove that it was self-defence, I would be going straight to jail, and knowing Alex, who had the gift of the gab, he would talk his way out of any possible conviction. I didn't care any more about us being brothers; those ties were now long gone. My mother and father had tried to change my mind by lecturing me about family and how you should always love your own blood like you love yourself, but I had given them enough chances. My father had the chance to change this narrative by approaching Alex long ago, but he was weak and never took the opportunity. Alex had the chance to confess his sins to all, especially to my uncle, who was his one devoted supporter. His time had also run out. No more excuses, no more lies, no more hiding. I was preparing Bethany and Priscilla for battle when the phone rang. With Bethany the bat clutched tightly in one fist I answered the phone, "Hello. This is the police. We received a call from your line and for safety precautions we must attend your residence to ensure there is no one there in harm." I wasn't ready for them to come as I needed to calm myself down. So, I told them to come in 40 minutes as I wasn't home. I was waiting outside the house when they arrived not long after. They asked me a series of questions, to which I explained that it was just a brotherly quarrel. I couldn't tell the truth, that I finally had the chance to dance with a blood devil, they would think I was insane. So as calmly as possible I lied to them, while they nodded their heads, took the details quietly and left.

Not long after the police had left my residence, my mother rushed downstairs to frantically share some news. "Michael, your brother is in the hospital. He said he felt like he had a heart attack, so they are keeping him for observation. We must keep your brother in our prayers and let go of all this hostility." I rolled my eyes, this was typical Alex behaviour; whenever he was faced with the possibility of confrontation he staged some dramatic situation that would victimise himself. He was a coward to the core, never able to deal with the consequences of his actions or own up to his mistakes. I was surprised hearing the news from my mother, I expected Alex, the con artist and mastermind of manipulation, to be far more creative than that. Heart attack, ha, he must be getting rusty. So, with Alex in hiding, I spent the weekend just waiting to jump at another chance for confrontation. Desperate to get more allies, I informed my father of the incident at his company. Still freshly wounded from the not only embarrassing, but also extremely infuriating 'case of mistaken identity' encounter, I was ready to tear down the city. But in the case of my father I knew what to expect. He arrived home Monday evening eager to inform me it was just a simple case of mistaken identity and told me not to be hot-headed because there are always two sides to a story. I shrugged; I had no more words to say to a man who had let me down so many times throughout my life. I was ashamed for my father, he had no integrity, no pride; he was basically just an old mat lying there for everyone to trample over. That was everyone except for me, who he wouldn't believe in a case where I had proof. I was done trying with my dad, so I told him, "I've had enough. I am leaving, fuck this. I'm taking my wife and daughter with me, we can't be around this drama and these lies anymore." I had attempted to leave several months ago when my brother had decided to come for a visit to bring his new girlfriend home.

Acting as though nothing was wrong, he put on a sickening act in front of his now fiancée. "Oh Mikey, tell Sophia about the times we used to organise dance competitions with the kids in the neighbourhood." I just stared at him, he knew very well that we had never done that together. That had been me and my younger sister, he was just using our experiences to impress his now *fiancée,* and I just couldn't handle my horrible brother, who had never stopped once in his life for a second to ask me how I was doing, now acting like we had ever shared some sort of bond. He was brushing off all the damage he had previously inflicted, erasing the pain he had caused, it was as though he genuinely believed that he had been a good brother to me. Well, that was his prerogative, he could continue to believe his own lies while I started to collect all the proof I needed to prove my innocence. Watching his sickening front that he was performing for his fiancée, I was repulsed. Who was he? I sat there and observed him, even when he tried to engage with me I just stared. "Michael, Michael?" I couldn't hear the words but as I stared at his face, I could see his lips form the words, his face scrunching up in frustration. I was in a trance; I knew that this act was the last straw.

The next day, I decided to confront my uncle to get a serious response to my letter. Driving to the company, I started to think about what I would say; I was anxious to think of how my uncle would react. Parking my car, I walked up to the office where I noticed the two managers who had almost attacked me standing in the corridor leading to the office. They were deep in conversation with my uncle who was another partner in the business, and his son, my cousin Anthony. I slowly walked up to them, waving hello in Anthony's direction, a spiteful gesture, as he had mistreated me for quite some time. Keeping up appearances, which is the most important thing to maintain in Arabic culture, I gave him the customary kiss on the cheek and a hug hello stating, "I know you don't like me and that's okay, but you are going to listen to the series of events that took place last Thursday. After being treated like a complete criminal in the family office, I was beyond embarrassed and ashamed, then to top it all off when I went home and told my father what had happened, he accused me of being aggressive and being the instigator of the problems." I paused and waited for Anthony to say something, but he remained silent, just staring at me, so I continued, "After the incident, no one apologised to me, they just informed me that it was a case of mistaken identity, and that they were told that an angry customer was coming to the office and had threatened the staff. I don't know how it was possible then for it to be a simple case of mistaken identity when I had called the reception desk five minutes prior to my arrival and confirmed my visit with my auntie. The two managers who had confronted me would've been sitting in the office with her during that phone call, so clearly someone informed them that I was coming and just wanted to scare me away." Anthony still sat there, speechless while I pleaded my case. My uncle was standing a few metres away, observing with an amused expression but not quite listening. "Also, if there was a threat, how come my cousin didn't come out of the office to check and see who the client was as it would've been someone he had been consulting with. The staff do not have a right or shouldn't attack anyone without a director or owner's consent, as the owners have a legal right to protect the staff and witness any events that may lead to violence. There is a legal requirement for a duty of care, so what happened with me does not make any sense."

I turned to face my uncle, his face was swelling up in anger as he spoke, "Stop shit talking. What do you want? What are you doing here? Just stop shit talking." His words were spoken with such animosity, it was as though I was the lowest form of human being on this planet. He would've addressed a thief, and adulterer, a murderer with more respect than he just did with me. By this time, around 14 staff had started to huddle around him, witnessing him abusing and disrespecting me, as if I hadn't already had enough. Even though I was still a shareholder of the company they seemed excited at the prospect of confrontation. They wanted a show, well I would bring it then.

As I started to leave, I stopped in front of the office, turned around and screamed my uncle's name out with the anger of years of built up aggression, "Uncle Charlie, fuck you. Fuck this family, fuck this business and our family name. I am no fucking bikie." Then I pulled out my ID and waved it around wildly in the air yelling, "I am not changing my name, I am still a fucking shareholder, but you are not my family anymore. I have my wife's family, my Tonga family now who treat me better than any of you have been, like I am one of their own." I then gestured towards my uncle with my middle finger and said, "You see motherfucker. I wasn't threatening to tell you the truth, not in a manner of physical violence. But mark my words now, let me make it clear that in the future you will never disrespect me like the way you have ever again."

That night I arrived back home, expecting my mother to tell me she had been inundated with calls from Uncle Charlie, or the manager who had blatantly lied to my father about not threatening me at the office. She hadn't, but to my extreme surprise a few hours later my uncle showed up at my house. Had he come to disrespect me even further, in my own house? I watched from the window as he pulled up slowly in his yellow Peugeot convertible; he was not alone. He got out of the car, and as he did the manager exited too, looking around cautiously, as though entering enemy territory. Now this is what you would call a dead man walking. They both came to the front door and knocked, I answered immediately. "Mikey how are you?" My uncle's voice trembled as he spoke, as though he didn't want to be speaking to me, but knew it had to be done. "We have come here to tell you that we are both very sorry for what happened at the office. We would like to make amends and move past this family drama." He held out a box of expensive Cuban cigars: a peace offering. I remained silent for a few minutes, basking in the pleasure of watching him squirm at having to apologise to me. I knew he was dying inside, and I wanted to savour every moment of it. He had disrespected me for several years prior, so he really deserved a lot worse. The punishment didn't really fit the crime in this scenario, but I had to take what I could get. Thoughts flooded back reminding me that he had never visited me and my wife in hospital when we had our baby, and after that he had never even congratulated us. I had to let go of these grudges and accept his peace offering. Taking the Cuban cigars, I replied, "That's okay, but you disrupted me and disrespected not only me, but my entire family. I accept your truce, but you don't have worry about seeing me around as I am never going to the family business or any family functions ever again."

Twenty-four hrs passed since my uncle's apology, and it was if that one event had opened the floodgates for the rest of the family. My mother received endless phone calls and apologies, as though she was the one my uncles had caused pain to over the years. Not ideal, but at least they were admitting that they were wrong. My father began to acknowledge my existence again as his son, calling me by my old nickname 'Mikeboy', and asking me to help him with projects around the house. More than anything I was happy for my daughter. She was the reason why I needed to make peace with the family, I had a legacy that I wanted to leave her, and I could not do that with a tarnished name. Alex always stated that the past should be left in the past to justify his years of sin and wrongdoings. However, I was an innocent man being accused of crimes I did not commit. Just like Jesus who was crucified for sins that he never committed; I decided to resurrect myself and take one for the team.

Evil Will Always Win at the End

The spaceship catapulted high up into the air, landing upside down on the carpet floor. "Astronaut John are you alive?" I tapped on the ship, waiting for some sign of life. Nothing. "Nooooooooo!" I wailed, "Astronaut John is dead!" I ran around the room, arms in the air mourning for my deceased toy. "What are you doing?"

Alex was standing in the doorway, giving my six-year-old self an unimpressed look. "Mikey, you're too old to play with these stupid toys. It's time you became a man." And with that he walked over to my bright-yellow toy spaceship, picked it up and smashed it against the wall repeatedly, while I watched in horror as my favourite toy shattered into pieces before my eyes.

Sitting at my dining room, pen in my hand, these were the memories that flooded back to me. I needed to release the years of horror, let it all go, and writing about it was my only solution. Weeks after my re-acceptance back into the family, I realised that nothing had really changed. The apologies had come in from my family to my parents, but to me there was no acknowledgement of any wrongdoings. I still felt like an outsider, the only difference was that now I wasn't being abused, just ignored. Tapping my pen against my blank pad, I realised that I didn't know where to begin. How could I convey the brutal truth that my brother was completely evil? Yes, his gambling and lies really did not help, but the addictions he had were just mere warning signs about his true nature. He enabled his vices and let them take over because he was selfish. The chance for a fresh start passed him by many times and he didn't even look its way. I thought about his fiancée, who was completely blinded to his past; she really had no idea what she was getting herself into. The second time she came with Alex for a visit to my parents' house it was as though she worshipped the ground he stood on. Gazing adoringly at him when he spoke, silently watching him move around; her eyes never left his sight. There was however, one moment where Alex slipped up and for a split second revealed his true self. We were at the dinner table and Alex's fiancée was asking him if he wanted to try some of my mother's fish, her specialty. "No thank you, darling. I will try the lamb instead." A few minutes later, the fish was being passed around again, and naturally she passed it onto Alex, even though he had declined once before. Staring at the fish and then his fiancée, Alex snapped, "What did I tell you before? I don't want any fish. My God you are exhausting sometimes." She went instantly quiet, clearly embarrassed, sitting there with her head facing her lap. At that moment, I hated my brother even more, he could even find faults in the sweetest person, someone who would do anything for him. Thank God I would never have to see his face again. The cat was out of the bag and no one could force me to have anything to do with that horrible human, if you can even call him that. The only time I would accept having to be anywhere near him would be at my mother and father's house if he arrived unexpectedly or at a funeral involving the passing of a family member. That's if he didn't die in the next few months, as I desperately hoped. Holding a grudge this strong isn't healthy; it can turn your insides black and make the skies stormy and grey. I carried a hate so intense that I couldn't think clearly, I could barely focus on anything other than seeing Alex fail, or die. Looking up at the family portrait that was hung on my parents' walls from when we were kids I felt a slight pain in my stomach. Was it a pain of guilt, knowing that I just could never forgive Alex? You see family defines who we are and what we are. You are supposed to take the good with the bad and then move on. Forgive and forget blood is stronger than any quarrel or fight. But with my brother it was all bad and there was nothing that could be said or done to make me forgive him. I had vowed to myself to make it a lifelong commitment to never forgive him, as ties were now finally cut. The revelation had come to me: No one had the right to sabotage your life or your relationships with others just because they share your DNA. I looked down at the first two words that I had written on the blank paper, *Never forget*.

A few weeks had passed, and the family stood still; Alex hadn't attempted to contact me to make amends, he just continued as though nothing had happened. Alex had done it again, played my entire family while they just sat on the fence trying to support both of us. Awkwardly running between the two of us like little lost baby chickens chasing after their mother. One morning, I decided to approach my father about how to break this ridiculous situation. "I just don't know what to do, I need to move forward from all this but I don't know how to when everyone is just sweeping the past under the rug." My father sat silently, stirring his herbal tea slowly and gazing out the kitchen window. Without turning to face me he spoke, "Michael patience is a quality that you have never had. With patience will come everything you need, and all your questions will be answered." Frustrated I let out a large sigh and walked off, my father had never been of any help when it came to issues with Alex. He preferred to stay clear of any conflict and just wait it out. Well, I had waited long enough. I had waited far too long to clear my name, far too long to regain some sort of respect within the family, respect that should have never been taken away from me. I was going to take action, I just didn't know how yet.

Around 2 am the next morning, I was woken up by a banging noise coming from downstairs. Looking over at my wife sleeping peacefully I decided to go investigate on my own. Putting on my dressing robe I made my way cautiously down the stairs. The kitchen light was on. In the dead of the night I could hear every creak and crack, every sniff and shuffle. Someone was in there. Feeling anxious at the unfamiliar noises and foreign presence I slowly crept into the room. What on earth? As if watching a surreal film, I was confronted with one of the strangest sights I had ever encountered in that house. There was Alex, sitting at the kitchen table, his face buried in a pile of cocaine. "Alex?" At the sound of my voice his head immediately froze, then jolted to look at me. His eyes were bloodshot and tired; it was as if he hadn't slept in weeks. After evaluating my presence, he turned back to his plate of drugs and started snorting again. "Alex, stop it! What are you doing?" I cried out to him, in shock at a side of my brother I had never seen before. It was as if he was under a spell. He buried his face even further into the pile of white powder; I wasn't even sure how he was breathing. I walked over to him and grabbed his hair, "Alex, stop this! You need help." Pulling his head up out of the drugs I was confronted with the sight of gushing blood pouring from his nose. "Oh my God, Alex." I covered my mouth in shock at the blood mixed with cocaine that was dripping from his nostrils. He didn't respond, just stared at me, eyes wide open, not blinking.

Then he started laughing, hysterically screaming two words, "I'm dead. I'm dead." Over and over again, he pulled his face closer to mine crazily yelling, "I'm dead. I'm dead. I'm dead. I'm—" shaking, something was shaking me.

"ALEX," I screamed, waving my arms frantically.

"Michael, shhhh you're having a bad dream. Calm down." My eyes started to focus on my surroundings, where I saw my concerned wife staring at me.

"Huh, Alex? Where is he?" I was confused, Alex's crazed face was still fresh in my mind.

"Babe, Alex isn't here. You were having a nightmare. You woke me up when you started screaming something about being dead. It scared the shit out of me." Still reeling from shock at the horror I had just witnessed, or thought I had witnessed, I tried to snap myself out of it and focus on calming myself down. I just couldn't get Alex's insane eyes out of my mind, the intense hunger that drove him to almost killing himself with drugs, it was imprinted in my brain like nothing had even been before. I tried to go back to sleep but like so many nights before I ended up just lying there, almost paralysed in fear of the idea of shutting my eyes. I didn't want that tormented scene to come back to life, I would stay awake for the rest of my life if it meant never having to witness what I had seen ever again. The next morning, I was a zombie, I had barely shut my eyes since waking up from that nightmare. Something still felt terribly wrong, and I didn't know what it was, but I knew that I needed to call Alex. Picking up the phone I realised I had no idea what I was going to say to him. I still hated him, nothing had changed there; I just needed to hear his voice. I just needed to know that my dream hadn't been real.

"Hello?" Alex's fiancée picked up the phone. Her tone sounded strangely desperate

"Hi, it's Michael. Is Alex home?"

"Michael. I was just going to call you. Alex hasn't been home the past two nights. I have no idea where he is or if he's okay. Has he been in touch with you?" I went silent, something was wrong, I could feel it. I didn't want to convey my worried thoughts to Alex's fiancée, who was already panicking so I just acted calm.

"I'm sure he is fine, have you tried calling any of his friends?"

"I have no idea who he hangs around these days. He's just been so secretive lately." Her voice was soft and trembling, as though she was on the verge of tears. This was not a good sign, Alex being secretive and going missing meant most likely one thing; he had fallen victim to gambling once again. I knew the haunts that he frequented, so once I got off the phone and convinced Alex's fiancée not to worry, I quickly got dressed and headed out. I made my way to the Lucky Lady Casino, a small run-down spot that Alex used to be a member of. Walking through the swinging doors, paint peeling and hinges creaking I felt immediately out of place. Inside it was as though there was no sense of time; the fluorescent lights swung back and forwards, providing a continuous artificial light source, masking the fact that there was not one single window in sight. The clientele was mostly greying old men smelling of musty cigarettes and the occasional widowed housewife dressed in track pants and crop tops that were too tight for their figure. I glanced around the room, scanning for a familiar face; instead, my gazes were received with empty, lifeless eyes that wouldn't look away. Was this where souls went to die? I asked myself. I had enough of this place, even the air in here felt thinner. I began to make my way to the exit when I caught a glimpse of someone sitting with their back towards me, wearing a very familiar jacket. It was an oversized leather jacket with 'Make Love, Not War' painted onto the back, I could tell Alex's favourite jacket from anywhere. I walked over to where my brother was sitting playing the pokies and grabbed him from behind.

"Alex, really? I thought you had gotten over this dead-end lifestyle. You know your fiancée is at home worried sick about you." I was angry and frustrated; I had to come to Alex's rescue once again, after everything. Alex remained silent, focusing on the machine and pressing the button to play.

"Are you even listening to me? Alex?" His lack of movement or acknowledging that I was even standing there was infuriating me. I could feel my blood starting to boil, years of tension building up again. "After everything you've done to me, you're going to just ignore me when I'm trying to help you?" Finally, he turned around and just stared at me, his clothes were dirty and stained, his hair ruffled as though it hadn't been washed in days.

"Everything you've done for me? What the fuck have you ever done for me except try and steal my life?" Alex stood up, screaming. He was clearly high on whatever substance had been keeping him awake for the past few days. I looked at him with pity; this was clearly a man with no hope, a man who had nothing going for him. The sad thing was, everyone around him had just continued to give him handouts his entire life, and he still couldn't cope. "What the fuck have you done for me?" he repeated, bringing his face close to mine, as though he was challenging me. For the first time in my life I genuinely felt sorry for him, he would never be happy, he was tormented from the inside out. He would spend his life searching for meaning, searching for something that could fill the large gaping hole in his soul, but nothing would ever suffice. His hunger would really kill him one day, his desire to fix himself by drugs and other addictions would just end in his demise. Alex was a demon that was created by my parents' karma for disowning their first-born. He was a demon that sucked the life of every living being around him, and I had to walk away. I was starting to realise that I would never get the answers I wanted, never get the closure I needed, but that was okay. After seeing Alex at his most rock-bottom, I was happy just to move on.

I looked at Alex and said, "You're not worth this mate," and then made my way to the exit.

A few days had passed and despite thinking I had reached a resolution within myself, I still couldn't stop thinking about Alex and what had gone down. Had he gone home yet? I hadn't heard anything from his fiancée, so I assumed that he was back home, for now anyway.

That night I was sitting at the dining table when all my family's phones started to buzz and sound simultaneously. First my father's, then my mother's and so on, until every phone had buzzed including my sister's and her husband's, who were visiting for the evening.

My wife's expression of anger towards me was hurtful, she stared at me in the most disappointed way, her eyes glaring at me as she huffed and puffed aloud.

"Michael, you promised me!"

"You swore you left him alone at the casino!"

"Michael, who are you, you're not the man I thought you were!"

It was like deja vu all over again. My complete family turning against me.

The only soldier I had to fight this war with was my mother. She refused to accept the accusations, over the years, eye witnessing besides me what Alex was capable of. Due to a mothers love she could never admit her son was evil but would always question where his character or behaviour came from, either genetics or a power from beyond! There she stood, fighting for me, debated with everyone knowing that I would never strike close death on Alex. Even if I verbally threatened violence against him in my moment of anger or rage, even if I said I wanted revenge, she knew just as I did that I would never go through with it.

I guess Alex's only brick wall was our mum. But due to her weakness of being over empowered by the clan, she simply went quiet towards the end of the heated argument. She was tired and old. She had nothing left, no will power to fight back. Sitting there in her favourite green arm chair, staring at the floor. Silent.

Then silence filled the room, but I guess there is always silence before the storm.

My father raised his arms and began to yell at the top of his voice. Screaming, his face turning red, fuelled with hatred.

"Get out, get out, look what you've done!"

Whilst waving the phone of Alex's bloody bruised photo in front of me, I glimpsed at the text and began to read in disbelief,

LOOK AT WHAT MICHAEL DID...

I was dumbfounded, I don't know why but I couldn't speak. I opened my mouth trying to defend myself in some way, but no words followed. Maybe because I knew that they wouldn't believe me. I turned to my wife for some support and even she was staring at me like I was a stranger. They were all staring at me, even my beautiful darling daughter; her eyes wide in shock after accidentally seeing the image of Alex's broken face.

I knew I wasn't welcome there anymore, there was nothing I could say, so I just picked up my jacket and walked out. Getting into the car I realised I didn't really have anywhere to go. Alex would've sent the photo out to all my friends and family, who would've sided with his manipulative self as usual. I got in the car and drove to the one place I knew would accept me, the bar. I had been sober for a while, after years of depression and using alcohol to mask it. But now I had been pushed to the edge, Alex had framed me; he had made me out to be a psychopath and everyone believed him. There was no hope left anymore, I needed that drink more than ever. One drink turned into five, which turned into eleven, and then I was kicked out. I couldn't stop drinking, the liquor was helping me to forget about the horrible fact that my own brother was the devil, yet everyone thought that it was me. My car keys were blurry, but I needed to drive home. I had to talk to my wife to tell her that I hadn't done it, she would believe me; she knew everything I had been through in the past with Alex. Getting into the car I couldn't stop thinking about everything that had happened, from the day I had been born up until now, Alex had made it his plan to make my existence a living hell. I hated him, with every inch of my being, I hated him and wanted him to die. I was past the point of drunk, I was delirious and could barely see anymore. The traffic light colours all blurred into one, yet somehow, I managed to make it home. Walking through the front door I paused, stumbling, yet feeling overcome with rage. I had stopped to look at the family portrait that hung in my parents' hallway. What a joke, all smiling faces, when the fact was that all of us were dead inside because of Alex. He was a virus that had infected the entire family, he had spread into the passageways, into every family member's airways, taking over their consciousness and convincing them that he was good. He needed to die, but what would be the best way to kill him? I could strangle him to death, that would be really satisfying, watching the life slowly drain from his body. Or I could shoot him with my parents' rifle, that would be a funny twist too, considering it was the same rifle I had tried to finish myself with a few months ago.

As I attempted to walk downstairs leading to the main dining room, I slipped, tripping and hitting my head on the rail. In a drunken state of mess and with the pain that I received from the fall, I simply blacked out only to be woken by loud screams erupting from the dining room entry, snapping at me, awakening me out of my deep drunken sleep.

Through my blurred vision, I looked down at my hands: red, so much red, where was it all coming from? "Michael, what have you done now?" My father was standing at the foot of the stairs, staring behind me in horror. I didn't understand, what he was referring to. I turned around to where he was looking, to find a figure slumped on the floor, draped in one of Alex's jackets. Wait, it couldn't be? I know I had been thinking about killing him, but had I gone through with it? I had been so lost in my thoughts I wasn't even conscious. Had I really killed my own brother? I was still extremely intoxicated and could barely stand up; I felt as though I was going to vomit, from the liquor, not from the sight of the body lying on the floor. I was numb, but not for long as my confusion was slowly replaced with joy. Alex. Was. Dead. The words danced around in my head vibrantly, filling my entire body with electric rhythms of ecstasy. I hadn't felt this happy in my entire life; Alex's existence had been a heavy weight wearing me down since the day I was born. I had never known this feeling of lightness, this feeling of being finally, free. Then a sharp voice pierced through the silence in the room. That voice, that disgustingly familiar voice that made my heart drop instantly.

Alex had walked into the room from the side entrance, screaming, "Michael why, Michael not our mother! How could you?"

I replied in anger, "I didn't, I didn't! Not me."

Alex pounding his closed fist into a wall, with a thundering voice replied,

"Look at your body…you animal, all covered in blood. Look at your hands, all bloody!"

Alex kept screaming, his lies filling the room.

"I found Mum dead in the kitchen and you drunken asleep in the dining room!"

"Police have been called, Michael."

"You're the Devil. Devil Son and Devil Brother."

"May you burn in hell."

I slumped to the floor, drained entirely of all life. There she was, my mother. Eyes closed, as though she were eternally asleep, peacefully resting like the angel she was. My favourite person in the whole world lay dead in front of me, she was the only one who had stood by me my entire life and I had lost her. Suddenly a pair of hands grabbed me from behind and started choking me.

"Michael, you killed her. You killed your own mother! You killed my wife!" My father now had me on the floor, the entire weight of his body being pressed onto my windpipes, as I gasped for air. I wasn't fighting back; there was nothing to live for. Somehow, I had killed my mother and now I was going to die, just as I deserved, or did I?

Or DID I?

The panic of the trauma just kept me silent. As the room started to go hazy, I caught a glimpse of Alex's tattered face out of the corner of my left eye. Watching my father choke me to death, he was smiling, an eerie smile of satisfaction. We locked gazes and he gave me a sly wink, and then everything went BLACK.

CPSIA information can be obtained
at www.ICGtesting.com
Printed in the USA
LVHW081934160320
650193LV00017B/397